'You took a

Holly flashed [illegible] calculated guess, Doctor. I didn't make any promises. As for Dougall Walsh—or anyone else who comes to my door—if I think they have a condition that requires medical attention, my advice is always that they consult a doctor.'

'And what the hell makes you think you're qualified to make that kind of judgement?' he rasped. 'How dare you jeopardise the lives of my patients?'

She faced him, breathing hard as a wave of dizziness swept over her. 'I'm a doctor,' she forced out.

Jean Evans was born in Leicester and married shortly before her seventeenth birthday. She has two married daughters and several grandchildren. She gains valuable information and background for her medical romances from her husband, who is a senior nursing administrator. She now lives in Hampshire, close to the New Forest, and within easy reach of the historic city of Winchester.

Recent titles by the same author:

SOMEONE ELSE'S BABY
TAKE A CHANCE ON LOVE
A PRACTICE MADE PERFECT

HEART IN
HIDING

BY
JEAN EVANS

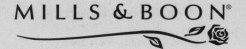

MILLS & BOON®

First published in Great Britain 1999
Harlequin Mills & Boon Limited,
Eton House, 18-24 Paradise Road, Richmond, Surrey TW9 1SR

© Jean Evans 1999

ISBN 0 263 81835 7

Set in Times Roman 10½ on 11½ pt.
03-9911-52774-D

Printed and bound in Spain
by Litografia Rosés S.A., Barcelona

CHAPTER ONE

THE overnight storm had died down at last. Now, gradually, as the November morning wore on, rain turned to snow—light, powdery flakes, driven by an increasingly bitter wind.

Holly Hunter glanced at the leaden sky and shivered as she bent to toss a log into the dying embers of the fire.

'It looks as if winter's here, Mac.' Stooping before the flames, she coughed slightly as she stroked the warm fur of the terrier who lay gazing up at her.

As if in response to her words he raised his head, making a soft growling sound in his throat.

Holly smiled ruefully. 'I know. I'm not looking forward to going out either, but we'll make the best of it, won't we, boy?'

The Westie sat up, the sound in his throat deepening as he looked at the door. Holly frowned as she quietened him gently with her hand, tugging her cardigan more tightly around her as she straightened.

'What is it, Mac? Is someone out there?'

She scarcely needed to ask. The little Westie was a good house dog. No one came anywhere near the cottage without her having good warning of it and, sure enough, seconds later someone tapped at the door.

'Stay, Mac.' She issued the softly spoken command as she went to open the door, gasping as she let in a shaft of cold air that ruffled her dark chestnut hair and stirred a cloud of smoke from the chimney.

'Fergus! What on earth are you doing out on a morning like this?'

Fergus Campbell, his face tanned and weathered by sixty Scottish winters, handed her a box. 'Maggie sent over some eggs. She said you'd no doubt be finding a use for them.'

Holly smiled at the offering. 'Will you tell Maggie it's very good of her? I'm very grateful.'

'Och! It's no bother.' The man's breath fanned white into the air as he hesitated. 'Well, I'll be away, then.'

With a wry half-smile, Holly stepped back. 'I was just about to make a pot of tea. Will you come in and have some before you get back?'

'Is it the herbal scenty stuff?' Fergus advanced cautiously and she grinned as he made his way over to the fire.

'Not unless that's what you want, Fergus.'

'No, no.' He waved the suggestion away, bending to fondle Mac's ears. 'The proper thing will be fine.'

She filled the pot and reached for two mugs. Adding milk and sugar, she poured the brew and handed it to him.

He winced as clumsily he took it from her, manoeuvring the mug between swollen fingers.

'The hands are no better, I see.' Holly frowned. 'I would have thought the treatment should be working by now.'

'Aye, well...' Fergus Campbell shifted uncomfortably and Holly fixed him with an accusing stare.

'Fergus, you did *go* to the doctor?' She saw the faint colour rise in his neck. 'Didn't you promise me a month ago?'

'Och, I didn't like to be bothering the man.'

'Fergus! He's there to be bothered.' Setting her mug down, Holly stifled a sigh of exasperation as, very gently, she took one of his hands in hers. She felt him tense as she studied the swollen joints.

'You have arthritis, Fergus. Ignoring it, won't make it go away.' She could feel the heat of inflammation in the affected joints and could guess at the pain he must be suffering. 'The doctor can give you something to relieve the symptoms. Go and see him.'

Carefully he withdrew his hand but she had already guessed by the stubborn set of his face that she was fighting a losing battle.

'I dare say the young chappie is fine, but I'll be waiting until Alex Douglas is back from his sickbed.'

'But that could be months, Fergus, especially if it was a heart attack. I've heard his partner is good at his job.'

'Aye, well, maybe, maybe not.' He slanted her a glance. 'Maggie reckons the stuff you gave her cured her cough in no time at all. Can't you find something among those potions of yours…?'

Holly shook her head. 'Fergus, the mixture I gave Maggie was nothing more than a natural brew of honey and lemons. It wasn't a miracle cure,' she explained patiently. 'The recipe was handed down to me by my granny. Anyone could have made it. Maggie knows that.'

She frowned. 'You need to see the doctor, Fergus. He can help you. I'm not a miracle-worker.'

'There's some in these parts wouldn't agree.' Fergus put his empty mug on the table, before tugging up the collar of his jacket and edging his way to the door. 'I'll be away, then.' He hesitated. 'Arthritis, you say?'

She smiled slightly. 'See your doctor, Fergus. I promise you, he can give you something to ease the pain.'

'Aye, well…' He sighed heavily.

Holly opened the door and coughed as the chill air gusted in, stirring up the smoke again. When he had gone she set about tidying the small kitchen, before tossing another log onto the fire.

Mac lay with his head on his outstretched paws, his black, bright eyes watching her every move. As she straightened up his ears cocked, alert to the possibility of a walk at last.

Holly bent to ruffle his white coat. 'What?' She grinned, pushing him playfully. 'Oh, all right, then. Yes, it's your turn now. Let's go and see what we can find today, shall we?'

Five minutes later, with Mac scampering at her heels, she was heading for the small bay and the water's edge.

In the past hour a weak November sun had finally broken through the clouds, cutting a shining track across the sea. The wind whipped at her hair and her skin felt clammy as she pushed the errant strands from her eyes.

Digging her hands into her pockets, Holly took a deep breath, coughing a little as she picked her way over wet boulders. She laughed as Mac peered inquisitively into a pool, before bounding after her.

She loved the isolation of the place, the weather's ever-changing moods—through the gentleness of summer to the wild, sometimes violent rages of the sea in winter.

She paused for a moment, shading her eyes to gaze at the wild coastline, experiencing the same delight at the scene now as she had eighteen months ago when she had first arrived in Glenloch.

Usually, after a storm at sea, she would walk the shoreline, collecting pieces of driftwood which had been washed up, but today there was nothing to replenish her already rapidly dwindling supply of winter fuel.

'Oh, well, nothing for us today, Mac.' Coughing again as the wind caught her breath, she turned to retrace her steps.

With the Westie bounding ahead of her, she made her way slowly back to the cottage. The sun had disappeared behind the clouds again and as the light began to fade the wind seemed to have an added chill to it.

It was a scene she had become accustomed to, but no

matter how many times she walked the rugged coastline she still never failed to be stirred by its changing beauty. And to think that she had come here by chance, upon a whim.

As she walked, Holly reflected with a wry smile on the reaction of her colleagues and friends when she had suddenly announced her intention to give up her job and her nice, modern flat to live in a small croft on the coast of Scotland, miles away from the nearest town.

Their reactions had been almost laughable. She had guessed that, secretly, several of them had envied her. Most had made no secret of the fact that they had thought she had been completely mad. But, in fact, it had been the easiest decision she had ever had to make and not for an instant had she regretted it.

She had needed a fresh start, a chance to offload some of the emotional baggage she had seemed to have been carrying around of late, so that when she had seen the croft advertised in a glossy magazine she had acted on impulse. She had written for details and then promptly forgotten about it until the large envelope had thudded onto her mat a few weeks later.

She had known at once that it was everything she had been looking for. It had been her chance to start again, or at least to give herself a breathing space. Within a month the contract had been signed.

Not that it didn't come as something of a shock when she finally arrived to take up residence, with all her worldly goods—and Mac—tucked into the one small hired van.

The driver left her standing amongst her few possessions—those she had chosen to bring with her—hesitating as if half expecting her to change her mind. And for a few seconds she *did* panic, seeing the bare stone walls, a gap in the roof.

But she stayed, and, though basic, the croft served her few needs well enough, despite the lack of facilities, especially when, as now, the weather was getting colder.

The climb up the narrow track left her feeling breathless and coughing and she paused briefly to press a hand to her ribs, waiting for the painful spasm to pass.

Mac, who had gone on ahead, came back to her, waiting uncertainly at her feet.

'It's all right.' She smiled. 'I must be out of condition. I'm coming. I suppose you want your dinner?'

Minutes later she was within sight of the croft. A faint but welcoming plume of smoke drifted from the chimney.

Holly paused for a moment, shading her eyes, then she froze. The door of the croft was open, yet she was sure she had closed it. Something—someone—was down there. Holly could feel the sudden dryness in her mouth.

As if sensing her sudden tension, Mac gave a low, rumbling growl.

'All right, Mac,' she murmured, shivering as she edged her way slowly forward.

Easing the door open fractionally, she peered inside. It took a few seconds for her eyes to adjust to the darkness. There was no sign of movement.

Shakily, her fingers fumbled for the oil lamp and the matches she always kept close by. If only she had thought to light it before she'd gone out.

'I had a feeling you'd be back pretty soon.'

The distinctly male tones, coming from behind her, made her jump. Turning quickly, Holly felt the breath momentarily catch in her throat. It was the shock, she told herself, of discovering an intruder in her home.

She exhaled painfully. Brushing a damp wisp of hair from her forehead, she stared at the man. As he moved slowly from the shadows she could see that his face was attractive, strong and ruggedly chiselled.

He was tall, around six feet—that much she could judge even from where she stood. His hair was dark, almost black. He looked tired and there was the faint shadow of dark stubble on his chin.

The match she was holding flared slightly in a draught, burning her fingers. Powerful shoulders moved beneath the jacket he was wearing as he reached over to take it from her, extinguishing the flame. The brief contact seemed to reinforce her sense of panic as the man's hands closed over her frozen fingers in a firm grip.

Her shoulders made contact with his tautly muscled chest. For several seconds, it seemed, she was held within the circle of his arms as he leaned forward. She held her breath as he took the matches from her.

'I think you'd better let me.'

He turned slowly, and she edged back unsteadily as he straightened up in the pale circle of light cast by the lamp. She was conscious of every line of his tall frame, from his shoulders beneath the open jacket and denim shirt to a slim waist and lean thighs beneath the faded jeans he was wearing.

There was something compelling about the tanned features, along with something else—something vaguely unsettling.

She stood, transfixed, feeling her colour deepen as he seemed to take in every detail of her too-slender figure and delicate features.

It wasn't just the overwhelming sense of power that seemed to emanate from him as he stood there, it was the look of barely suppressed hostility in the blue eyes that took her breath away, even though she could think of nothing she had done to deserve it.

She faced him, breathing hard. 'Perhaps you'd be good enough to tell me what you're doing here, in my home? I don't remember inviting you in, or maybe you make a habit of invading other people's privacy?'

His glittering gaze narrowed briefly. 'The name is Callum McLoud. I'm the doctor over at Glenloch Surgery. I took over as senior partner when Dr Douglas had his heart attack.'

'I know who you are,' she cut him off sharply. 'This is a small community, Dr McLoud. Nothing happens but that everyone knows about it within twenty-four hours. There aren't any secrets.'

'Some seem to have managed better than others,' he said in a glacial tone.

'I don't gossip, Dr McLoud. I like my privacy and I respect other people's. Which is obviously more than can be said for some.'

Shivering, she bent to throw a log onto the fire, and coughed as it crackled into life. Her chest ached and her skin felt clammy. She ran the back of her hand across her forehead, wishing Callum McLoud would just go and leave her alone.

Without a word he took the basket of logs from her as she straightened up. Holly averted her eyes from his hands. They were strong and tanned. Dark hair shadowed his wrists as he stacked the wood in the hearth.

'You still haven't said why you're here.'

'I thought it was time we had a talk. In fact, I'd say it's long overdue, wouldn't you?'

He pulled back the curtain and peered out of the window, before turning slowly to look at her. 'This place is freezing and I'll lay odds the roof leaks. How the hell do you manage to survive?'

Well, really! Holly's mouth tightened ominously. Wasn't it enough that he had walked in, uninvited? 'I do just fine, thank you, Dr McLoud. Not that it is any business of yours.'

A muscle flicked in his hard jaw as his gaze took in the single chair, the few books she had brought with her.

'Doesn't it bother you that people talk?'

'Why should it?' She turned away to set a pan of water on the fire, brushing the dust from her hands. 'If people choose to gossip I can't stop them.'

'And you don't care what they say?'

She gave a slight laugh. 'Why should I? It does no harm.'

Shrugging herself out of her jacket, she went to hang it on the peg and was disconcerted to find him watching her. She could only guess what she must look like.

She didn't need a mirror to see that she had lost weight over the past few months. The jeans she was wearing had seen better days and her naturally curly brown hair hadn't seen a hairdresser since she didn't know when.

'I like my life the way it is,' she said, striving to keep a steady tone. 'It suits me. I leave other people alone, they usually leave me alone. I prefer it that way.'

'Doesn't that rather smack of running away?'

Really—the man was insufferable. Holly fixed him with a cool, green stare. 'Then obviously I haven't run far enough.'

Callum McLoud slanted a glance over her pale features and seemed annoyed by what he saw.

'I'm glad you find it amusing.' His dark gaze narrowed. 'What you do with your own life is up to you,' he said coolly, 'but when I hear that you've taken it upon yourself to treat my patients then it becomes an entirely different matter. I'm here now to warn you that it must stop.'

Holly stood, feeling the hot colour surge further into her cheeks. 'Are you threatening me, Dr McLoud?'

The arrogant mouth twisted. 'Oh, I don't make threats, lady.'

'I have *never* treated your patients.'

'Are you denying that you gave Maggie Campbell medicine?'

'Indeed I am,' Holly uttered furiously, her green eyes flashing fire. 'The only thing I ever gave Maggie was some common-sense advice and the contents of a jug of lemon and honey made for my own use. If people want to create a mystery there's nothing I can do to stop them.'

His frowning gaze swept over her and there was a glint in the blue eyes which might have been intimidating if she hadn't been so angry. 'But you do and say nothing to prove them wrong.'

'Why should I?' She faced him, breathing hard. 'Why should I have to defend myself? How I choose to live my life is my own affair.'

'Not when it affects my patients.' His voice was ice cool. 'Dougall Walsh insists you gave him an ointment that "sorted out my back in no time",' he quoted tersely. 'I had him in my surgery two days ago, demanding to know why I couldn't prescribe the same stuff.'

'Dougall Walsh had nothing from me that he couldn't have bought over the counter in any chemist's shop. It was a simple herbal remedy.' She paused for breath, wincing at the sudden pain in her side.

'Perhaps he also forgot to mention that I gave him some good old-fashioned advice as well,' she went on hotly. 'I simply pointed out to him that if he will insist on sawing logs when his back is playing up then he is asking for trouble, and it was no good looking to me for sympathy.'

Her mouth tightened. 'I told him to let his good-for-nothing son earn his keep for a change.'

Blue eyes regarded her with an unreadable expression. 'Are you also denying that you told Cassie Brewer that her baby would be a boy? How could you possibly know that? A crystal ball, maybe?'

Holly laughed scornfully, then winced as a spasm of

coughing overtook her. 'I hate to disappoint you, Dr McLoud. It was nothing so technical.'

He frowned and she flashed him a look. 'Cassie's mother had four boys before Cassie came along. Her aunt had two boys, her sister had two boys. I'd say the odds were pretty high on Cassie's baby being a boy, wouldn't you?'

He gave a slight laugh. 'You took a chance.'

'I made a calculated guess, Doctor. I didn't make any promises. As for Dougall Walsh—or anyone else who comes to my door—if I think they have a condition that requires medical attention, my advice is always that they consult a doctor.'

'And what the hell makes you think you're qualified to make that kind of judgement?' he rasped. 'How dare you jeopardise the lives of my patients?'

She faced him, breathing hard as a wave of dizziness swept over her. She moistened her dry lips with her tongue, wishing that she could sit down if only for a few minutes. But she wasn't prepared to give him that advantage.

'I'm a doctor,' she forced out, wondering vaguely why the room was spinning.

This time the dark eyes narrowed cynically. 'You mean you're practising?'

'Not struck off, if that's what you mean.' Involuntarily she reached out as her head began to swim. She heard Callum McLoud swear softly under his breath.

A glass was thrust into her shaking hands. 'Here, drink this.' She was vaguely aware of him frowning.

Right now she wasn't even sure whether she was still capable of standing unsupported. Her legs seemed to have turned to jelly.

She swayed and was held instantly, drawn against the taut muscular body. He was close, too close. She could smell the faint undertones of the aftershave he was wearing.

'Dammit, woman! you must know you have a fever. Why didn't you say you were ill?'

It was galling to discover that her hands were actually shaking as, breathing hard, she tried to draw herself up and free of his grasp. The last thing she needed—or wanted—was sympathy.

'I am perfectly well, thank you, Dr McLoud,' she declared roundly, before slumping gently to the ground in a dead faint.

CHAPTER TWO

HOLLY lay fighting the mists that seemed to be clogging her brain. Her chest ached and she felt sick. What had happened? One minute she had been holding a perfectly normal conversation and the next...

'Oh, no!' She groaned as dawning memory slowly returned, bringing with it the vague realisation that Callum McLoud was bending over her and taking her gently in his arms.

With a cry of protest she made a feeble attempt to stop him. 'What are you doing?' Weakly she tried to push him away. Her voice seemed to be stuck somewhere in her throat as she struggled dizzily to sit up.

'I'd take it slowly if I were you.'

The warning came too late. Callum's mouth twisted wryly as he watched the tide of colour wash from her cheeks. With a groan of dismay she pressed a hand to her mouth and sank back against the pillows.

'So you've decided to come back to us.'

She swallowed hard. 'What happened? Where am I?'

'Don't you remember?' His brow rose quizzically. 'I was trying to help you to sit up.'

Holly peered at him warily from beneath her lashes. Her mouth felt dry. She felt awful and probably looked worse. 'I must have fainted. If you just give me a minute...'

He stood looking down at her and then, as she pressed a hand to her throbbing head, moved to draw the curtains, letting in the light. His mouth was grim as he returned to study her pale features.

'You're at my cottage.'

She stared at him. 'Your... I don't understand.'

'You've been ill. I could hardly just walk away and leave you. Oh, don't worry.' He had seen the sudden hint of panic in her eyes and his mouth twisted. 'My house-keeper, Mrs Clarke, has been clucking like a broody hen, keeping a watchful eye on you.'

He turned to the tray set on the bedside cabinet. 'I thought you might manage to eat some hot soup.'

'I'm not hungry.'

'You'll eat anyway.' He set the tray in front of her and plumped up the pillows, before reaching for the spoon and practically forcing the liquid down her throat. 'Mrs Clarke made the soup specially. I'll not have her feelings upset.'

Callum McLoud was a bully, she decided, but she felt too tired to argue.

'All right, I can manage. I'm fine,' she protested as she began, reluctantly, to eat, only to discover to her surprise, as the soup slid down her parched throat, that she was actually hungry after all.

She ate most of it, before lethargically pushing the dish away. 'I'm sorry. It was lovely but I can't manage any more.' Even so small an exertion seemed to have left her feeling exhausted.

As if aware of it, he removed the tray. 'Aye, well, you've not done so bad. You're still very weak, but there's nothing that a few more days' rest and some good food won't put right.'

She stared at him through eyes which suddenly seemed ridiculously to be full of tears. 'I still don't understand what happened, why I'm here.'

'You collapsed. Here, you'd better take these.' He thrust two tablets into her hand, followed by a glass of water.

She eyed them suspiciously. 'What are they?'

'Antibiotics. You had pneumonia.' He looked at her and his expression darkened. 'Surely you must have realised?'

'I've had a bit of a cough for a while, that's all.'

'A *bit* of a cough! *Dammit*, woman, you could have died.'

'Rubbish!' She peered witheringly in his direction. 'Don't you think you're being a little melodramatic, Dr McLoud? I really don't—'

A muscle flickered in his jaw. 'Have you any idea just how long you've been here?'

Holly stared at him, trying to dismiss the sudden qualm that rippled through her. She moistened her lower lip with her tongue. 'I… I'm not… A few hours?'

His brow rose quizzically. 'Try three days.'

'Three days!'

His mouth tightened ominously. 'I can't believe you weren't aware of any symptoms. You've had a fever, over one hundred and two degrees. You've probably been coughing up blood and there must have been chest pain.'

How could she deny it when there had been all of those things and more? The fatigue, the shortness of breath after even the mildest exertion. It had happened so gradually that she hadn't noticed. Or maybe she hadn't wanted to see.

She stared at Callum McLoud. She sensed his anger but she hadn't asked him to come barging his way into her life, taking charge. Why couldn't he just have left her alone?

'Look, I'm sorry.' She licked her dry lips. 'I didn't intend this to happen. I'm grateful for what you've done, but if you'll just bring me my clothes I'll get out of your way.' She pushed back the covers, struggling dizzily to sit up.

'I really wouldn't do that…'

The words came too late. Callum swore softly under his breath as he watched the colour fade from her cheeks as she tried to stand. She groaned with dismay as she slumped weakly into his arms.

'You crazy little fool. I did try to warn you.'

Holly subsided weakly against the pillows again as he helped her back into bed. She closed her eyes, pressing the back of her hand against the throbbing in her temple. If only the room would stop spinning.

'I won't impose on your hospitality a moment longer than is necessary. I don't imagine your wife is too happy at having a total stranger descend on her like this.'

'It's no problem,' he said evenly. 'I'm not married. I was engaged once but it didn't work out.' He smiled briefly but didn't enlarge on it, and Holly found herself wondering briefly if his failed engagement had put him off the institution of marriage altogether and left him preferring the bachelor existence.

'I'm sorry. I didn't mean to pry.'

'Don't worry about it. I just wanted you to know that you can take all the time you need.'

It was a tempting thought, to lie here in the warm, soft bed, feeling safe—cared for.

'You've been very kind.' Her chin rose stubbornly. 'But I'll get out of your way. I just need a day or so, that's all.'

'Must you always be so damned independent?' he bit out tersely.

'I don't need your pity, Doctor.'

'That's just as well because I'm not offering any.' He straightened up and she saw the cool amusement in his eyes. 'Unfortunately, as a doctor, I do have a certain obligation.'

Well, really! The arrogance of the man. She closed her eyes firmly in a determined effort to shut him out of her sight as well as her thoughts, only to open them again on the startling realisation that Callum McLoud was fumbling with the buttons of her pyjamas. Correction, *unfamiliar* pyjamas.

'What are you doing?' She slapped him away. 'How

dare you?' Breathing hard, she tugged the sheet up to her chin. 'What kind of a doctor are you…?'

'A very busy one.' He sighed deeply and held up a stethoscope. 'In God's name, woman, you're perfectly safe. I only want to listen to your chest. I'm not lusting after your body.'

Her cheeks flamed. She may not be looking exactly her best, but did he have to be quite so insulting?

'There's nothing wrong with my chest, thank you very much,' she ground out.

'I'll be the judge of that.' He detached her clenched fingers briskly from the sheet, brushed her jacket aside, applied the stethoscope and stared fixedly at her chin.

Her breath caught in her throat as she looked at him, her eyes widening, focusing with renewed clarity on his tautly honed features, on the firmly moulded mouth that hovered just inches from her own.

He was attractive. The thought rushed crazily into her brain. Not that she was interested in Callum McLoud—or any man, come to that.

'Just breathe deeply and slowly.'

Deeply was fine. It was slowly she was having trouble with, especially as his fingers brushed coolly against her skin.

She stared at his head. The scent of aftershave drifted to her nostrils. Her eyelashes clamped firmly closed. She was delirious, that was it—feverish.

'You're doing just fine.' He straightened up, frowning. 'You're much better but you still have a way to go.'

And she would be on her way like a shot if he would just let her get out of here. The thought hammered inside her head as she scrambled, with undignified haste, to re-fasten the buttons.

'I'm feeling much better,' she lied feebly, in the hope

that he would go, just leave her alone to be ill in peace and recoup her strength.

He made no move. Instead he looked down at her, his mouth grim as he studied her pale features. 'What beats me is how you could have let yourself get into this state. Why didn't you ask for help?'

'Because I didn't need or want help,' she flared angrily. Why couldn't he just leave her alone? 'I didn't ask you to interfere...'

'Well, that's tough,' he said tersely. A spasm flickered across his features, leaving them taut. 'What the hell were you trying to prove?'

She closed her eyes again, thinking briefly of Tony. She had been doing just fine until this man had come along, interfering in her life.

'You've been neglecting yourself.' The accusation came.

Holly opened her eyes to stare at him, noting for the first time the tiny lines of exhaustion around his eyes and mouth, and she sensed that while he might be hard on those around him Callum McLoud was no less hard on himself.

Her mouth tightened. 'What I do with my life is none of your business.'

'You *made* it my business.' His eyes narrowed in sudden frustration. '*Dammit*, you claim to be a doctor. If that's true, how could you be so irresponsible? How much weight have you lost recently?'

'I haven't—'

He gave a small laugh. 'Have you looked in the mirror lately? It's not a pretty sight.'

She glared at him, her feminine senses stung by the realisation that he found her unattractive. He was hateful, she told herself. She didn't give a damn what he thought.

She was spared a reply as someone tapped at the door

and the housekeeper bustled in, her fact lighting with pleasure as she saw the almost empty soup bowl.

'There now, you're looking brighter for a little food. Oh, Doctor.' Her glance went to Callum. 'There's a phone call. It's Jim Prescott. His mother is suffering with her knees again. I said you'd have a word.'

He was already striding towards the door. Holly watched, breathing a small sigh of relief as it closed behind him.

She had just closed her eyes again and sunk back against the pillows when it opened again abruptly.

'You'd best be drinking some tea. You need to keep up your fluid intake. And *don't*—' he emphasised the word, as if she were a recalcitrant schoolgirl '—even attempt to get out of bed unless someone, preferably me, is here to keep an eye on you.'

He looked at his watch. 'I've a surgery to take. Try to eat something more if you can, and then sleep. I'll look in later.'

A quelling look from Callum Mcloud's quick backward glance silenced the reply on Holly's lips. He really was too much, she thought weakly. Arrogant *and* a bully.

The door closed again. This time she kept her eyes firmly open.

'Well, I'll be leaving you to rest, then.' Mrs Clarke smiled as she went to open the door. 'Oh, and there's someone here to see you. He's been very patient.'

Not another visitor, Holly thought. I can't bear it. Then she heard a scampering of paws and Mac was suddenly hurling himself at the bed.

'Mac, oh, Mac. Is it you? Where have you been?' Her eyes filled with ridiculous tears.

'Now, you're not to be fretting.' Amy Clarke lifted the struggling Mac up onto the bed. 'The wee chappie has been fine. In fact,' she confided softly, 'I think the doctor has quite enjoyed having his company in the evenings so you're not to worry yourself.'

'I feel I've been such a nuisance. I just need a little time and I'll get out of your way.' Without being aware of it, she sniffed hard, feeling more tears well up to sting at her eyelids.

'There now.' Amy Clarke smiled. 'Don't you take what the doctor said too much to heart.' She crossed to the window to twitch the curtains neatly into place, before turning to pour a cup of tea. 'The poor man's been worrying himself to death. Why, he sat here through the night while the fever was at its worst.'

The tea was wonderfully refreshing, Holly thought, sipping at the hot, sweet liquid. She had forgotten just how good it was. She looked at the older woman. Callum McLoud worried? Now that she found hard to believe. Annoyed, maybe, but worried?

More disconcerting by far was the thought that he had sat beside her bed, watching her.

'We'll soon have you right as ninepence again.' Smiling, Amy Clarke gathered up the tray. 'You're not to rush things, not on my account. It's nice to have someone to fuss over, what with the doctor out all hours.'

She sighed heavily. 'I tell him he works far too hard, but he says it's the job he chose to do and he'll not change, more's the pity. Still, you get a wee rest now. Here's the bell. Just you ring if you need anything.'

Her pillows plumped and finally, blissfully, left to her own devices, Holly dozed, waking an hour later to the realisation that it was dark and that, Callum McLoud or no Callum McLoud, she had to get to the bathroom.

Which was easier said than done, she realised as, pushing back the covers, she managed to sit shakily on the edge of the bed.

Her legs felt as if they belonged to someone else, but

she had absolutely no intention of ringing the bell. She had suffered enough humiliation to last a lifetime where Callum McLoud was concerned. She would get there on her own even if she had to crawl on her hands and knees.

It didn't quite come to that. It needed a real effort of will to force herself to get out of bed and make it as far as the bathroom, where a quick glance at her reflection had her groaning with dismay. Her face looked pale and drained and there were dark shadows beneath her eyes.

'He's right,' she muttered, looking at Mac. 'It's not a pretty sight, is it?'

Having got this far, she decided to make the most of it, and minutes later she was standing under the shower, her head tilted back, her eyes closed as the needle-sharp points of water sprayed over her body.

It helped. Cautiously brushing her hair, she purposely left it loose. Whatever the tablets were that he had given her, they had certainly had an effect.

By the time she had dried herself and managed with difficulty to struggle into a robe she found hanging on the back of the bathroom door, she was actually beginning to feel more human.

With Mac at her heels she wandered back to the bedroom, but she felt too restless simply to climb back into bed. Instead, strengthened by the soup and the tea, she made her way towards the stairs.

The house was quiet. With a bit of luck Callum had gone out on a call. The thought cheered her as she made her way hesitantly—and holding securely onto the handrail—down the stairs.

It was a large cottage—stone-built. Shivering, she went from room to room in search of Amy Clarke, hesitantly pushing open doors.

She came to an abrupt halt as, frowning, Callum

McLoud pushed aside a pile of papers, rose to his feet and came towards her.

'What the…? I thought I told you to stay in bed.'

'I couldn't,' she said flatly. 'I needed to go to the bathroom.' She swallowed hard. 'I was looking for Mrs Clarke. I…I couldn't find my clothes. I hope you don't mind, I borrowed this.'

She hugged the robe more securely around her, the colour rising faintly in her cheeks as his hard glance flashed over her slender figure. Suddenly, illogically, she was aware of how little she had on beneath it.

She thought he was about to say something because his whole body was still for an instant and his lips parted slightly. Involuntarily, she shivered, and, as if instantly aware of it, he stood aside, allowing her to enter.

'You'd best come to the fire,' he ordered tersely. 'Warm yourself before you manage to undo all the work we've done so far.'

She headed for it, holding her hands out to the blaze. As she did so, her gaze swept over the study, taking in the sturdy, lovingly polished furniture and heavy velvet curtains at the window. Shelves of books lined the walls. A single lamp cast a glow over the large desk, its surface covered with papers.

'Do you always work this late?'

'It's a busy practice. Since Alex had his heart attack, Jamie and I have been covering as best we can. It's just a damn nuisance that it's come at a time of year when we're always rushed off our feet with the usual viruses, not to mention a flu epidemic.'

He moved to shift a pile of magazines and she found herself thinking that he looked quite different, quite good-looking even in a rugged sort of way. It might have been the fact that he had had a shave, or the fact that he was wearing a dark suit instead of the faded jeans and sweater she remembered. He seemed younger than she had first thought—probably around thirty-five, she guessed.

Absorbed in her own critical survey, she suddenly became aware that his own deep-set blue eyes were appraising her in return, and it was a surprisingly disconcerting feeling.

Her hand went to her throat. 'I haven't exactly made things easy for you, have I? I'm sorry.'

'Forget it.'

If only it were that easy.

His gaze narrowed. 'You'd best sit down before you fall down.' Pouring a small glass of sherry, he pressed it into her hand. 'Here, drink this.' He stood over her, watching as she sipped at the drink. 'You're still very pale. You need feeding up.'

Holly sighed. 'I don't need a lecture, Dr McLoud.'

'So you've said.'

She toyed with the glass, tilting her head back. 'Well, you don't need to concern yourself on my behalf any longer, Doctor. Just as soon as I can get my things together, I'll be on my way.'

'The name is Callum,' he said. 'And have you taken a look outside recently?' He nodded in the direction of the window. 'There's a couple of inches of snow out there and winter's hardly started. Just how long do you think you'll survive?'

'It's not your problem, is it?' She forced a smile. 'I meant what I said. I'll be out of your way by tomorrow.' She put her glass down and headed for the door.

'Holly, wait.'

She heard him swear softly, but she refused to listen. 'I'll be just fine. Don't you worry.' She turned to fling the challenge as she headed for the door, only to find that her feet had somehow become tangled in the robe, and she stumbled.

Her breath caught sharply in her throat as she collided with his powerfully male body. Her lips parted on a gasp as he reached out to steady her, bringing her close so that her nostrils were invaded by the fresh, clean, musky smell of him.

The sensuous mouth was only a breath away. Shock briefly widened her eyes as she stood, mesmerised, by the surge of totally illogical sensations that coursed through her.

She heard his soft intake of breath. 'Are you all right?'

His hands held her arms, turning her to face him when she would have moved away. His touch sent tiny shock waves darting through her. She drew a deep breath, her face taut with strain.

'I...I'm fine.' She stiffened, trying to pull away, and saw him frown before he released her abruptly.

'You'd better get some rest. We can talk about you leaving when I think you're strong enough.' He had turned away, dismissing her even as her lips formed a protest.

Pausing in the doorway, she looked back, but he was already engrossed in his work again. As far as Callum McLoud was concerned, she was just a nuisance he could well do without.

Well, he needn't worry, she thought crossly as she made her way up to her room. She was every bit as eager to leave as he undoubtedly was to see her go. As far as she was concerned, that couldn't come a moment too soon.

Which made it all the more galling to discover that he was right. She was still incredibly weak, and it was three days later before she finally felt strong enough to make her way to the Glenloch surgery.

She had toyed with the idea of simply leaving a note, before making her way back to the croft, but it had seemed too cowardly. Whatever she might feel about this man, the very least she could do was see him face to face and thank him.

She arrived to find a full waiting room and a harassed receptionist attempting to deal with a young mother of a fractious two-year-old.

'If you'd like to take a seat, Mrs Crawford, Doctor will see you as soon as he can.' Fiona Stewart smiled as she reached out to silence the telephone, cupping the receiver with her hand.

She smiled apologetically at Holly and added another name to the list. 'Sorry about this, we're rushed off our feet. Yes, hello. Mrs Benson? Is it young Hamish still with the cough? No, the doctor hasn't forgotten. He's still taking surgery but he'll get to you as soon as he can. Aye, that's fine.'

Replacing the receiver, she looked at Holly. 'You'll be wanting to see Dr McLoud?'

'Yes, well, that is—'

The phone rang again. Reaching for the list, the girl smiled wryly. 'I'm afraid you might have to wait a wee while.' She lifted the receiver again. 'Hello? Mrs Robertson?' She frowned sympathetically. 'Oh, the poor thing. No, you bring him to the surgery. Doctor will make time to see him.'

She made a note on the pad, her brown eyes twinkling as she looked at Holly. 'Sorry about that. I swear, every child in the school has gone down with the spots in the past twenty-four hours.' She consulted the list again. 'I'll pop your name down and Doctor will see you as soon as he can.'

'Look, I can see you're busy.' Holly glanced at her watch and the crowded waiting room. 'It isn't important. Maybe I'll phone later.'

She had half turned away when Callum appeared in the

corridor that linked the consulting rooms. He was seeing one of his patients out.

'Try the tablets then, Mr Frazer. If they don't do the trick, come back and see me again.'

About to turn away, he glanced up. 'Holly?' He had removed his jacket to reveal a blue shirt. He looked tired. Worse than that, he looked exhausted, she thought. 'What are you doing here?'

She gave a slight smile. 'It's nothing. I just thought... I was going to leave a message.'

He frowned. 'Look, we can't talk here. You'd better come into my room.' He glanced at his watch, then at the girl behind the desk. 'Fiona, can you hold things up—just for a while?'

'I'll do my best.' She gave a wry smile. 'But they won't be happy.'

'Look, there's really no need. I can see how busy you are. I shouldn't have come.'

But somehow she found herself being ushered ahead of him into the consulting room. He motioned her towards the chair. 'Sit down.'

She shook her head. Where Callum McLoud was concerned, she thought better on her feet. 'No, really.' She looked at the desk, its surface littered with paperwork. 'I won't take up your time. I can see how hectic it is out there. I just came to thank you.'

'Thank me?' He shot her a quick, narrowed glance.

She moistened her dry lips with her tongue. 'I'm going home, back to the croft. I just wanted you to know that...that I'm grateful for what you did, but—'

'You can't wait to get away, is that it?' he said quietly.

'I didn't say that.'

'You didn't have to.' Humour glinted briefly in his eyes, and before she knew what was happening his fingers had brushed gently against her forehead.

She was aware of the tiny beads of perspiration dotting her brow. He frowned and his fingers closed on her wrist, searching for the pulse she knew would be hammering out of control.

It was completely crazy, but his touch was doing strange things to her, sending a wave of heat right through her, from her head to her toes, making the blood pound in her ears.

Startled, she met his glance, her thoughts spiralling dizzily through a haze of burning sensations that had nothing whatever to do with a fever and everything to do with the way his long, cool fingers brushed lightly over her skin.

'As I thought,' he murmured. 'You still have a fever.' He moved away and went to an open cabinet, leaving her to gather her scattered wits as best she could.

What was happening to her? It seemed she only had to be near him for her whole body to react, and it was a thoroughly unsettling reaction.

She shivered, watching as he removed a small bottle from the shelf, shook two tablets into a small plastic container and filled a glass with water, holding them out to her.

'Here, take these.'

'There's no need.'

'I think there is.' He placed the cup firmly in her hand. 'We've been through all this before, Holly,' he said smoothly. 'If you want a repeat performance...'

She swallowed the tablets, almost choking as she gulped them down. 'There. Happy?' She saw the tightening line of his jaw.

'If you want the truth, my professional opinion, then, no. I'm not happy about your going back to that place alone.'

'"That place" just happens to be home,' she retorted

sharply. 'And I'm perfectly capable of deciding what is best for me.'

'Are you?' His eyes glittered as he ran his glance over her pale features. 'I don't recall you made a particularly good job of coping. You need a proper diet and warmth.'

'So I'll eat and make a fire.' Yet suddenly, for the first time, she knew that she didn't want to go back to the croft, and she was shocked by the realisation.

It had been her refuge for two years—since Tony's death. She closed her eyes on the bleak memories and opened them again to look at him directly.

'I'll be just fine,' she said, rather more decisively than she felt. 'I didn't want to leave without at least saying goodbye.'

At the door she turned and said, 'I'm sorry I put you to so much trouble. I do appreciate that you didn't have to do what you did.'

'Even though you'd prefer it if I hadn't?' he said softly.

She tucked a strand of hair behind her ear. 'I'll never be able thank you properly, I realise that.' She gave a slight smile. 'Well, goodbye, Dr McLoud.'

It was disconcerting to find her hand shaking as she fumbled clumsily with the doorhandle.

Callum's arm came round her, the contact sending a kind of electric shock running through her. 'Here, let me.'

He was so close that she could see the firm texture of his skin, and she felt a tremor of something closely akin to excitement run through her.

No matter how much she might dislike his arrogance, there was no denying that he possessed an animal magnetism.

She straightened up, alarmed by the direction her thoughts had suddenly taken.

'Holly, wait.' He gave her a quick glance. 'There is a way.'

Frowning, she turned. 'I'm sorry?'

'If you meant what you said—about thanking me. There is a way.'

'I don't understand.'

'It's really quite simple,' he said evenly. 'I have a proposition to put to you. Why don't you stay? Join us at the practice.'

CHAPTER THREE

'YOU'RE not serious?' Holly stared at Callum incredulously, and gave a slight laugh.

His dark brows drew together. 'Never more so. You've seen what it's like out there. We're stretched to the limit.' He raked a hand through his hair. 'We're coping without Alex, but only just, and, as far as I'm concerned, that's not giving the patients a fair deal. We need help.'

'So why not bring in a locum?'

'Doctors aren't exactly flocking to the area,' he said drily. 'In case you hadn't noticed, we are a little off the beaten track. Besides, you know the area. You probably know most of the people.'

Holly smiled faintly. 'You mean I've probably practised witchcraft on most of them?'

Humour glinted in his eyes. 'I suppose I deserve that.'

'Oh, I'd say so.'

Callum's gaze narrowed as he studied her appearance, seeing the dark shadows beneath her eyes. His gaze roamed from the soft tumble of her hair to the generous curve of her mouth, her features devoid of any make-up, and the jeans and sweater which hung just a shade too loosely.

He said softly, 'You don't look old enough to be a doctor.'

'I'm twenty-seven, and I don't see that this conversation is getting us anywhere.'

'Maybe that's because you're not taking it seriously. I meant what I said, Holly. We could use you.'

She moistened her dry lips with her tongue, feeling a sudden sense of panic welling up inside her. 'It wouldn't work. You'll find someone else.'

'I don't doubt it.' He frowned. 'But it will take time and I don't want to wait until someone's life hangs in the balance just because we can't get to them in time. We need someone now.'

His eyes became glittering blue slits. 'Oh, but I was forgetting. You don't feel any sense of responsibility to the community you've chosen to live in, do you, Dr Hunter? It's far easier, safer, to opt out, isn't it?'

Holly almost choked. The man was insufferable. 'That's unfair.'

'Is it?' His mouth tightened briefly. 'Why don't you stop off at Reception on your way out? See how many visits I still have to make after I finish surgery.'

'I don't need this—' .

'No, nor do I. I got to bed at midnight last night, and I was called out again at five this morning, so, frankly, Doctor, your personal feelings of guilt don't concern me. My patients do. They deserve better than the standard of care we can give them right now simply because we're all too tired.'

She swallowed hard, then said slowly, 'Aren't you forgetting something? I...I haven't practised medicine for two years. You don't know anything about me.'

His mouth twisted. 'You said you weren't struck off. I know where you did your medical training. I also know that you were considered to be the best student in your group and that you passed your finals with honours.'

Holly gasped. 'You've been checking up on me.'

He laughed. 'Absolutely. You don't imagine I'd offer you the job otherwise? I do have the safety of my patients to consider.'

She swallowed hard. 'It still doesn't alter the fact that I'm out of touch.'

'You'll soon get the hang of things.'

She gave a sigh of exasperation. 'You're not listening to me.'

'I'm hearing every word. All I'm asking is that you at least consider the proposition. You could make a lot of difference around here—' He broke off as someone tapped at the door and a sandy-haired figure popped his head round.

'Callum, any chance of a word? Oh.' He glanced at Holly. 'Sorry, I didn't realise…'

'No, Jamie, come in. There's someone I'd like you to meet. Holly—Dr Hunter—Jamie Nichols, my partner.'

'Doctor.' Brown eyes twinkled as he came towards Holly. He was about thirty-five years old, of medium height and good-looking.

He extended a hand in welcome. 'Dr Hunter, this is a nice surprise.'

In spite of herself, Holly found herself smiling as her hand was clasped in a firm, warm grip. 'Dr Nichols.'

'Jamie, for heaven's sake. We don't stand too much on formality around here as a rule. Most of the locals know us far too well.' He grinned. 'There's no chance we'll be allowed to get too uppity.'

'In that case the name is Holly.'

'And very nice, too.' Jamie Nichols still retained his grasp of her hand. 'We must get together for a chat some time. I'm sure we'll have a lot to talk about.'

'I've been trying to persuade Dr Hunter to join us at the practice on a temporary basis,' Callum said. 'Just to ease the workload until Alex is fit enough to come back.'

Jamie grinned. 'Now, that sounds like the best idea I've heard in a long time.'

Holly shook her head. 'Look, I don't think—'

'Please, *please*, say yes.' He frowned. 'Seriously, I expect Callum's told you, we're all working on autopilot. I can't remember the last time I got a decent, uninterrupted night's sleep.' His brown eyes twinkled. 'Besides, it would be nice to have a pretty face around the place for a change.'

'Oh, thanks very much. I heard that.' Fiona, the receptionist, grinned as she tapped at the door and popped her head round. 'Callum, sorry to interrupt, but we've just had a phone call from Donald MacGregor's son. He says the old chap is quite poorly and he's worried. He wondered if you'd take a look at him.'

Callum frowned. 'Did he say what the problem is?'

The girl consulted her notes. 'Only that he started with a wee cough about a week ago, and now he's running a bit of a fever.'

Callum looked at his watch. 'I think I ought to go out to see him as soon as possible.' He glanced at the pile of cards on his desk. 'Can you call Andrew? Tell him I'll be over to see his father as soon as I can but it may take a while.'

'Will do.'

'I can see the rest of your patients, so long as they don't mind waiting a while longer,' Jamie offered.

'Are you sure you don't mind?' Callum raked a hand through his hair. 'Only I do feel a bit concerned. 'Donald is eighty-three and hasn't been so well recently.'

'We'll cope. Besides, from what I know of Donald, wild horses wouldn't get the old man to see a doctor if he had any say in the matter, so it must be pretty bad.' Jamie shook his head and smiled. 'You go. I'll manage here. You can owe me one.'

He glanced at Holly as he made for the door. 'Callum's right, we do need you. Of course, I'd be pleased to welcome you here on purely selfish grounds. Perhaps we can chat over a coffee. I'd be happy to show you around.'

Without turning her head, Holly could feel the weight of Callum McLoud's blue eyes watching her, a frown suddenly darkening his gaze. 'It's really not that simple—' she began.

'Didn't you say you needed to see me about something?' The set of Callum's mouth suggested that he was angry, and Holly felt the dull colour flood into her cheeks as she wondered why.

Jamie snapped his fingers. 'Ah, so I did. You remember the tests we did on Tom Baxter?'

Callum frowned. 'The fifty-year-old? He'd been complaining of chronic fatigue, chest pains, weight loss?'

'Aye, that's the one. Well, I thought you'd want to know the results of the tests came back this morning, and you were right.'

'Hell! Not TB?'

'I'm afraid so.'

Holly looked from one to the other. 'Surely that's pretty rare these days?'

'I wish that were the case.' Callum gave a wry smile. 'Unfortunately it's a misconception. The disease seems to be making something of a comeback.'

'But why?'

'It's simple enough. More people are living rough. I'll grant you it's a lifestyle some may choose, but there are some who genuinely can't find work, so they don't have money to spend on decent food. If you're undernourished, you're more susceptible. As a doctor, you'd know that.'

Holly frowned. 'It takes a bit of getting used to, that's all. I mean, it's something my grandparents knew all about, but in this day and age...'

'At least these days we have effective drugs and chemotherapy to deal with it,' Jamie said, 'so that the death rate from tuberculosis is practically nil.'

Holly frowned. 'Provided the bacilli don't prove to be drug-resistant.'

Blue eyes glinted as Callum shot a look in her direction. 'Well done, Dr Hunter. For someone who claims to be out of touch, you're not doing so badly.'

For some ridiculous reason the quietly spoken words sent a tiny frisson of pleasure running through her as she sent him a faint answering smile.

Jamie's mouth quirked as he held out his hand. 'Yes, well, time I got back before someone starts a mutiny out there. It's been a pleasure meeting you, Holly. I hope you're going to be around a lot more in the future. Callum's right—we could do with the extra help.'

The door closed behind him and Holly felt her gaze drawn involuntarily to Callum McLoud as he stood at the window, but his back was to her, denying her any glimpse of his expression.

'So, what do you say?'

She drew a deep breath. Everything was happening too fast. 'I need time to think about it.'

'Fair enough.' He turned slowly and she could feel his eyes studying her, without giving any hint in return of what he was thinking. 'In the meantime, why don't you come with me to see old Donald MacGregor?'

She stared at him. 'You want *me* to come with you? To see a patient?'

'Why not?' He dropped the case notes into his briefcase, snapping the locks closed before reaching for his jacket. 'The truth is, I'll be glad of some moral support.' He frowned. 'Ideally I'd like to get Donald admitted to hospital for a short spell. It would mean that his medication could be supervised and at the same time the family would get some respite.'

'He lives alone, doesn't he?'

'You know him?'

'Yes.' Holly frowned. 'Well, slightly. I don't think any-one knows Donald really well. We've met a few times when he was out walking his dog. We chatted. I got the impression he was lonely. I gather his wife died?'

'That's right, about three years ago. Her death hit Donald hard. He stopped looking after himself.' His mouth twisted. 'Andrew tried to persuade him to move in with them. It can't have been easy for them. Donald's not the easiest man to get along with.'

'Maybe he's happier where he is.'

'Maybe,' he acknowledged, 'but it's hardly practical. He wasn't eating properly. He became very depressed.'

Holly shot him a look. 'Maybe it's hardly surprising when everyone else seems to be making decisions for him. Did anyone stop to consider what Donald wanted?'

'They did what they thought was best.' A spasm flick-ered across Callum's face. 'It wasn't easy for any of them. It never is in that sort of situation. You must know that.' He frowned. 'Where do you draw the line between allow-ing an elderly, possibly infirm person their independence and showing a reasonable concern for their safety?'

'I don't know. Luckily, it's not a decision I've ever had to make.' Holly looked at him. 'I still don't see what you think I can do.'

'I'm not sure either,' he said evenly, 'except that I'm pretty sure I'm going to have a fight on my hands when it comes to getting Donald to agree to go into hospital. Someone has to persuade him.' He looked at her. 'He knows you. He trusts you. Will you come?'

Holly drew a shaky breath then nodded. 'Yes, all right. I'll come. As long as you understand that I won't do any-thing against my better judgement.'

'Fair enough. Come on, we'll take my car.' He gave a faint smile. 'By the way, where's Mac?'

'I left him at the cottage. I hadn't expected to be here so long. I'd planned to pick him up on my way home.'

'Ah, well,' Callum said easily. 'He'll be fine. It's Mrs Clarke's day to pop in. She'll spoil him.'

It was snowing again as she slid into the passenger seat beside him—dry, powdery flakes, falling from a leaden sky. As they headed along the coast road she studied him unhappily.

'You do realise I've agreed to come along only to give some moral support,' she warned. 'I'm still not convinced I can do anything to help—or even that I want to. You said yourself that Donald MacGregor can be stubborn. He may be over eighty, but he has a mind of his own and if he decides he doesn't want to go into hospital I won't stand by and see him bullied.'

A spasm flickered briefly across his features. 'I told you, I'm all for Donald retaining his independence, provided he can do it safely.'

He glanced briefly in her direction. 'Whatever you may think of me, Holly, I'm not a bully, but I'd be failing in my duty as a doctor if I didn't do what's best for my patient. Surely you can see that?'

She bit her lip and was still pondering the problem when they reached Donald MacGregor's cottage ten minutes later.

The door opened before they could reach it. 'Doctor, I'm glad you got here so quickly. He's through here.'

An anxious-looking man of about fifty led them into a small sitting room where Donald MacGregor lay on a bed. His head was propped against the pillows. His eyes were closed, his weather-lined face grey and drawn with discomfort.

'We moved the bed down here for him a couple of

weeks back when he began having trouble getting himself
up the stairs.'

'How is he?' Callum asked.

'Not so good, I think,' Andrew MacGregor said quietly.
'I suspect he's in pain, though he'll not say a lot.' He
glanced at his wife. 'Mary found him when she called in.'

'Hello, Doctor.'

Callum smiled. 'Hello again, Mary. I think you may
know my colleague, Dr Hunter?'

Mary MacGregor cast a look of curiosity in Holly's direction and nodded. 'Doctor, is it?' She picked up a cup
from the small table and looked at Callum. 'I made him
some tea a while ago, but he dozed off.'

'Has he eaten?'

Andrew shook his head. 'Not properly. Not for a few
days.'

'I bring his meals over,' Mary said quietly. 'He says
he's eaten them, but if you ask me the only thing putting
on any weight around here is the dog.'

The man in the bed stirred and she held his hand, patting
it gently. 'Dad, there's someone here to see you.'

Callum set his briefcase on the floor. Sitting on the bed,
he gently reached out to hold one thin, blue-veined hand,
his fingers automatically registering the rapid pulse.

'Hello, Donald. It's Callum McLoud. Can you hear me?'
He smiled as the paper-thin lids flickered open.

'Is it you, Doctor?' Donald blinked. 'I didn't expect to
see you.'

'I gather you're not feeling too well,' Callum said
gently. 'Andrew asked me to pop by to take a look at you,
see if we can't make you a bit more comfortable.'

The older man struggled to sit up, pushing weakly at
the covers, only to subside again as a spasm of coughing
left him distressed and breathless. 'They shouldn't have

bothered you. It's a wee bit of a cough, that's all. I'll be fine.'

Andrew looked at his father and shook his head, his face anxious. 'It's more than a wee cough, Callum. He's not getting any better.'

Callum nodded, his expression betraying nothing as he held Donald's hand. 'Donald, I've someone with me. A friend of yours.' He glanced at Holly, beckoning her forward. 'You know Holly. She's a doctor too.'

Holly smiled. 'Hello, Donald. I'm sorry to hear you're not feeling well.'

Watery blue eyes clouded with confusion. 'Can't breathe…'

She looked questioningly at Callum, and as he nodded she said gently, 'Can you tell me where the pain is, Donald?'

One hand fluttered weakly in the direction of his breastbone. 'Can't shift it. Tight…' He tried to reach the side of his chest.

'Don't worry about it, Donald,' Callum said. 'I just want to listen to your chest. Is that all right?'

He took the stethoscope Holly held out and she watched as he made his examination, the strong hands moving with surprising gentleness.

'You've got a bit of a rattle in there, Donald. I really think you need to go into hospital for a day or two, just to get you sorted out.'

The old man's eyes filled with tears. 'I don't want to go into hospital. I'll be fine here. Mary can look after me just fine.'

'I'm sure she can,' Callum said gently. He looked at Holly and she bent to put an arm round the thin frame.

'It'll only be for a few days, Donald. We need to get that cough sorted out. It's making you feel poorly, and you're not eating properly.'

'I'm not hungry.'

'No, I know.' She smiled gently. 'But you need to eat to build up your strength and at the hospital they'll be able to look after you, make you feel more comfortable. It'll only be for a few days and, I promise you, as soon as you're well enough you can come home again. But we do need to sort out the cough first.'

Callum shot a glance in her direction, nodding almost imperceptibly towards the door.

'You're worried about him, aren't you?'

He lowered his voice as they moved away fractionally. 'I think he's got an infection bubbling away in there, and it isn't going to get any better without help.'

Holly looked at him. 'What are you going to do?'

'I want to get him admitted. I could start him on antibiotics, but at his age and in his condition...' He frowned. 'There's too big a risk that it could turn to pneumonia and, frankly, I don't think he's strong enough to fight it.'

'How long do you think they'll want to keep him in the hospital?' Andrew asked anxiously as he and his wife joined them. 'And what about after that?'

'You've seen for yourself, he's not managing.' Mary voiced her concern.

'At the moment the chief priority is to clear the chest infection,' Callum said gently.

'It's bad, isn't it?'

'I won't lie to you. It could be.' Callum looked from one to the other. 'Physically he's in a pretty weakened state, and at his age pneumonia can be a killer. I need to get him to hospital where they can do blood counts and sputum cultures to identify the particular bacteria we're dealing with. He'll probably need X-rays, too.'

'He's not going to be happy about it.'

'No, I realise that. But I don't think we really have any choice, do you?'

Andrew looked at him. 'What are his chances of coming back here?'

'I can't give you any guarantees. Your father has always been a pretty strong character—that's in his favour.'

'Aye, he'll not give in without a fight.'

'The next few days will be critical. If we can just get him over that, get the treatment started and try to build him up, then we can be more positive.'

'I'd best sort out a few things he'll need to take with him.' Mary headed for the stairs.

Holly said, 'What about calling for an ambulance? Would you like me to do it?'

'You can use the mobile in my car, Holly?' Turning in the doorway, she almost collided with his solid frame. He stared down at her. She saw him frown. 'Thank you for coming with me. I do appreciate it.' His thumb brushed against her cheek.

Confused as a strange new sense of awareness brought the faint colour to her cheeks, she lifted her face involuntarily to his. 'I still don't think I'm really doing anything to help.'

'Sometimes it just feels good to have a little moral support, don't you think?' His hand came down briefly over hers. She swallowed hard, feeling suddenly ridiculously vulnerable.

She watched him stride away before she turned and hurried out into the advancing early winter darkness, glad of the cold wind that cooled her cheeks.

It was completely dark when, an hour later, the ambulance was finally on its way and they headed back to the cottage.

Climbing into the seat beside him, Holly leaned her head back and closed her eyes, feeling suddenly very weary.

Callum drove in silence and she was glad. Her head seemed to be spinning. She felt sad for Donald MacGregor.

He had led an active life and now, suddenly, when he was most vulnerable and afraid, he was being forced to leave everything and everyone familiar, and she had been party to it. The fact that it had been necessary didn't ease her feeling of guilt.

But it was more than that, she knew. It was a combination of things—concern for Donald and a sudden, disturbing awareness of her own increasing vulnerability where Callum McLoud was concerned.

In the darkness she watched him as he drove. Why was it that everything about this man seemed to have her nervous system leaping in chaotic disorder?

He was provoking and unsettling, yet she had been moved by his patience, both with Donald and the family. Not every doctor would have spent an hour of valuable time trying to reassure an elderly man, to persuade him to place his life in his hands.

Such strong, capable hands. Memories of their gentleness as he had touched her cheek sent an illogical rush of anticipation running through her, and she had to drag herself back to reality with a sigh.

'You're tired.' Callum turned his head to glance in her direction as they reached the cottage, and he brought the car to a halt, cutting the ignition.

She nodded. 'I don't know why. You did all the work.'

'Reaction. It's natural. Come on.' He climbed out and went round to open the door for her. 'We could both use some coffee.'

Mac greeted them, his tail wagging as they entered the kitchen. Callum bent down to tousle the dog's fur. 'Hey, hello, old fellow, I'm glad to see you, too.'

He flipped the switch on the electric kettle and reached for the cups. As he waited for it to boil he turned to look at her as she made a fuss of Mac.

'Donald is in the best place, you do know that?'

Holly smiled wryly as she went to sit at the table. 'I don't suppose he appreciates that right now.'

'Sometimes you have to make difficult decisions. There was no alternative.'

'You don't have to explain. I know it was the logical thing to do.' She looked at him and frowned. 'Look, I owe you an apology. If I seemed to imply—'

'Forget it.' He placed the cup of coffee in her hands, before lowering himself into a chair and stretching out his long legs under the table.

'I shouldn't have suggested that you would act out of anything other than the best motives where Donald was concerned.'

He gave a crooked smile. 'I don't always like what I have to do. It's not something that gets easier, you know. Sometimes there's just no choice. Having you there, it made it easier and I am grateful.'

His hand reached out briefly to cover hers. His touch had a strange effect on her, a sensation of instant fire that raced through her bloodstream and left her feeling dazed and bewildered.

Holly stared at him, bemused. The blue eyes returned her gaze steadily and he said softly, 'I meant what I said, about you joining the practice. At the moment we're hanging on by the skin of our teeth. You've seen what it's like. We're managing—just. But I don't know how we'd cope in a real crisis and I don't want someone to get hurt before we find out.'

She stared down at her cup. 'You make it all sound so simple.'

'Isn't it?' His gaze slanted over her. 'What do you have to go back to?'

She drew in a sharp breath. For the first time in a long time a sudden feeling of loneliness swept over her, threatening to overwhelm her in its intensity. Damn him! Damn Callum McLoud!

He raised his cup, sipping at the steaming liquid before setting it down again. His mouth hardened for an instant. 'It's a big, cold world out there, Holly. There are things we'd all like to run away from. Problems don't go away just because we choose not to face up to them.'

She purposely avoided his gaze, resting her elbows on the table with the cup between her hands. Her throat tightened painfully. He was right. What did she have to go back to?

He reached out to pour more coffee and for a moment she found herself staring at the dark strength of his arm. For one crazy moment she was tempted to reach out and touch it, as if in some way she could draw from it the power she sensed was hidden there.

Instead, shakily, she ran a hand through her hair. Maybe she wasn't as strong as she had wanted to believe.

His gaze honed in on the scar which was usually hidden beneath the natural wave of hair at her temple. His fingers closed over her wrist, halting the movement. 'How did it happen?'

Holly tensed involuntarily as he reached out, his fingers gently brushing her hair aside. She had almost forgotten it was there. In two years, what had been a raw wound had faded and thinned until it was now little more than a silver line.

'It…it was an accident. We were driving along the motorway at night. It was snowing heavily.'

She moistened her dry lips with her tongue. 'We were hit by another vehicle, a lorry. Our car left the carriageway and rolled down the embankment.' Her chair grated noisily as she pushed it away, getting to her feet. Mac, lying in front of the fire, lifted his head to watch her.

'Go on,' Callum said softly.

She swallowed hard, standing with her back to him to stare blindly out of the window. 'It's all a bit hazy. They told me afterwards that the other driver must have had a heart attack.'

Callum was on his feet, too, now. His hands on her arms forced her to turn and look at him. His voice was gravelly as he said, 'You said *we*.' And when she stared at him, '"*We* were driving along the motorway".'

She closed her eyes briefly, then opened them again. 'Tony, my husband.' She forced herself to look at him directly. 'He never regained consciousness. He died two days later in hospital.'

Some emotion flared briefly in the depths of Callum's eyes. 'I'm sorry. I had no idea.'

Sighing, she straightened up. 'There's no reason why you should.'

His mouth tightened. 'Was he a doctor?'

'A registrar. He enjoyed working in the hospital environment. It suited him.' She frowned. 'Tony finished his training a couple of years ahead of me. We met in medical school. He announced that he was going into orthopaedics.' She smiled slightly. 'That was what first attracted me to him. Tony was always so positive, so sure about what he wanted to do.'

'And what about you?'

'Me?' She frowned.

'You chose general practice.'

She shrugged slightly. 'I liked the idea of continuity, getting to know my patients.'

'You couldn't have been married long.'

'Just over two years.'

'I take it you have no regrets?'

Moving away from him, she gathered up the empty cups and took them to the sink. Rinsing them she set them on the drainer. 'About my work?' She turned slowly to look at him. 'No. I made the right choice for me. It was just…afterwards. I found it very hard to deal with. Couldn't deal with it.' She broke off, swallowing hard on the sudden tightness in her throat.

'It's all right. You don't have to go on. I shouldn't have asked.'

'It's all right.' She gave a shaky little laugh. 'I really don't know why I'm telling you. This is the first time I've talked to anyone about what happened.'

Callum bent to throw a log into the dying flames of the fire. 'You've never thought of going back?'

'No. Not yet. Maybe some time. I just felt I needed some time out.'

His mouth twisted. 'So there's no reason why you'll not be joining us at the practice for a while, then?'

She stared at him, fighting a sudden sense of panic. 'It isn't quite that simple.'

'Is it not?' Blue eyes met hers. 'Oh, but I was forgetting. You'll be wanting to get back. You've urgent commitments.'

Holly's gaze flew up to meet his and she found him regarding her with mocking amusement. Almost in spite of herself, she had to laugh.

'Even if I decide to join you, haven't you forgotten a few practicalities? In the first place, I don't have any transport.'

He straightened up and she saw the amusement in his eyes. 'Glenloch may be on the small side, but even here we do have the odd garage or two. I can always have a word with young Hughie McFadden. I'm sure he could come up with something.'

She felt the colour rising in her cheeks. 'All my belongings are still at the croft.'

'Well, obviously you'll not be going back there,' he said

evenly. 'At least not until the roof's been fixed and the water isn't coming in.'

The log crackled into flame and Callum turned to look at her. 'It just so happens that Alex's place is empty. He decided he'd convalesce with his son and family, and I know he'd be only too happy to have someone making use of it until such time as he decides he's ready to come back to us.'

Holly eyed him sharply. 'And where, precisely, is this place?'

'Oh, It's just a short walk away.'

'You mean…?'

'Aye.' His eyes glinted. 'We'll be neighbours, more or less. But I can put up with that. Provided you'll not have having any wild parties, that is.'

Holly choked. 'You seem to have thought everything out, Dr McLoud. You do realise that *if* I agree I'll only be doing it to help out, just until Dr Douglas is well enough to return.'

'That's all I'm asking,' he said evenly. 'So, do we have an agreement, then?' He held out his hand and, after a few moments' hesitation, she proffered her own. 'I'm not asking for a lifetime's commitment, Holly—just a few weeks, that's all.'

Holly knew the offer made sense. She might not like it, but he was right—the cottage wasn't in a fit state to go back to. She'd known it for a long time. She had simply put off doing anything about it.

'All right. Yes, we have an agreement.' At least it would give her a breathing space, time to think about her future plans. She stared at him and then, despite herself, she smiled. 'You drive a hard bargain, Dr McLoud. I just hope I'm not going to regret this.'

'The name is Callum. I'd like to think we can be friends.'

She drew in a deep breath as his hand closed over hers in a light but determined statement of possession, drawing her slowly, imperceptibly, closer.

She became aware of his frowning gaze, of the sensual mouth just a breath away, so close that her nostrils were invaded by the clean, musky smell of him.

She closed her eyes as his thumb brushed briefly against her cheek, sensing a strange riot of sensations running through her as his lips brushed gently against hers. He smelled of aftershave and danger, though she couldn't for the life of her have explained why.

She drew a deep breath, shivering slightly, and somehow, without her even being aware of it, he had released her.

He straightened up, frowning. 'It's late. You should have something to eat and get some sleep.'

Suddenly, frustratingly, Holly found that all trace of her former tiredness had vanished. Maybe it was the coffee, but suddenly she felt wide awake.

Picking up her jacket, she paused in the doorway. 'Well, I'll say goodnight, then, Dr McLoud…Callum.'

But if he heard he gave no sign as he turned away and began vigorously raking the embers of the fire.

Making her way slowly to her room, with Mac at her heels, it was galling to discover that her hands were shaking as she found the lamp and switched on the light.

What on earth had she let herself in for? She didn't know anything about Callum McLoud, except that he seemed to provoke a great many conflicting emotions in her, emotions she had imagined were safely under control—until now.

CHAPTER FOUR

OVERNIGHT frost had given way to a fine drizzle a week later as Holly set out on her first day in her new job.

Parking her car neatly in the car park, she reached for her jacket and new briefcase. She felt nervous. Eighteen months was a long time. What if she made a mistake—wasn't up to the job?

Well, there was only one way to find out. Drawing a deep breath, she locked the car door and headed for the surgery.

The waiting room was already crowded and the phones ringing as she made her way, carefully sidestepping a boisterous three-year-old, through to Reception.

'Morning. Sorry I'm late.' Breathlessly, Holly put her briefcase on the floor. 'I forgot to set the alarm,' she admitted sheepishly.

The move into the Douglases' cottage had been more exhausting than she had imagined. The fact that Alex had phoned to tell her to take all the time she needed had certainly made it easier.

If nothing else, it had meant she had avoided seeing Callum, although she had been well aware that she had merely been postponing the inevitable. But at least this way, when it happened, she would be more composed, better prepared.

'A couple of days will be fine,' she'd told Alex. 'It's not as if I have a great deal to move. In fact...' she had given a light laugh '...all my worldly goods will probably pack quite nicely into a couple of cardboard boxes!'

Which had proved to be a slight exaggeration, but close

enough to the truth to bring home a painful awareness of just what had been missing from her life in recent months.

In the event, she had fallen into bed feeling so exhausted that she had completely forgotten to set the alarm, with the result that she had overslept. So much for her determination to make a good impression on her first day.

Agnes Ferguson, the practice manager, greeted Holly's arrival with obvious surprise and relief. 'Oh, Dr Hunter, how nice. Dr McLoud said you'd be in some time. We didn't expect you till later on your first day, but I'm certainly glad to see you.'

Smiling, Agnes ruefully indicated the pile of patients' case notes. 'I'm afraid you're going to be thrown in at the deep end.'

'Hi.' Replacing the phone, Fiona scribbled a note in the diary before she looked up and grinned. 'I must say it's nice to see a friendly face around here.'

'Let's hope it says that way.' Holly smiled. She leaned over the desk to peer at the morning's appointment list and pulled a wry face. 'Perhaps it might be a good idea if I were to make a start.'

'Uh-oh. Here we go again.' Fiona reached for the phone, adding yet another name to the list as she spoke into it. 'That will be fine, Mrs Benson. You bring young Katie along to the surgery. Doctor will see her as soon as he can.'

Agnes handed Holly a bundle of cards and nodded ruefully in the direction of the waiting room. 'It's worse than usual because of the chickenpox, I'm afraid. I've never seen so many spots.'

'Oh, dear.' Holly glanced briefly at the list of names. 'I suppose the other doctors have already made a start?'

'Only Dr McLoud, but he came in early. Don't you worry now, we're only too glad to have another willing pair of hands. Shall I show you to your consulting room?'

'It's all right, thanks. I think I can find it. Dr Nichols showed me around last time I called in. Next to the treatment room, isn't it?' Holly waved and headed for the door. 'I'll manage. Just give me a couple of minutes then you can send the first patient in.'

All in all, her first morning passed remarkably quickly. Inevitably she saw several unhappy, red-eyed children, all obviously in the first stages of chickenpox. There was also a slipped disc, followed by a little light relief as Holly was able to confirm a pregnancy.

'Really? Are you sure?' Cathy Wallace was thirty-seven years old and had been married for eight years. Holly glanced at the notes on her computer screen, noting that the Wallaces had been trying, unsuccessfully, for several years to have a child.

She laughed as she washed her hands and returned to sit at her desk. 'Absolutely. Your test was positive, no doubt about it. I'd say you're about fifteen weeks.'

'Well, I'm blowed. And to think I'd been putting it down to a queasy tummy.'

'It's a mistake anyone could have made, especially under the circumstances.' Smiling, Holly glanced at the notes in front of her. 'I gather you've had some problems. I see that Dr Douglas referred you to a fertility clinic a couple of years ago.'

'Aye.' Cathy Wallace grinned, her cheeks flushed with excitement. 'Well, we didn't think too much of it when we were first married and I didn't become pregnant. You know how it is. Everyone tells you it takes time and it's nothing to worry about.'

She frowned. 'Only with us—with me and Tim—it just didn't happen, you see. And my mam had four of us, and my sister's got two boys, so I began to wonder if something was wrong with me or Tom.'

She gave a slight laugh. 'For a couple of years we

thought we were just unlucky, then we started to get a bit worried. We wanted a family, you see? That's when we decided to come along to see Dr Douglas.'

'Yes, I see. And he referred you to a specialist.'

'They did tests but they couldn't find anything wrong. They said there was no physical reason why I wasn't getting pregnant.'

'It can happen sometimes.'

Cathy Wallace smiled wryly. 'That's when we decided to adopt.'

'You mean…'

'That's right.' She chuckled. 'It took a while. There were procedures to go through. I don't mind telling you, there were times when we thought it would never happen, but then, eighteen months ago, we adopted a wee baby girl, Kirsten. She was just six weeks old when we brought her home.' She laughed. 'And now this.'

Holly smiled. 'It won't be the first time it's happened, that a woman becomes pregnant after adopting. It's possible the adoption, actually caring for a baby, gives some sort of kick-start to the hormones.'

'Well, whatever the reason, I'm thrilled to bits. I'm just wondering how I'm going to break the news to Tim.'

'I take it he'll be pleased?'

'*Pleased!* I'd say that'll be about the half of it. We thought we were lucky to get wee Kirsten, but now…'

Holly smiled. 'Well, the important thing now is to arrange for you to start regular antenatal care. You'll need to come to the clinic once a month to start with, and then more regularly as your pregnancy advances. I'll arrange for you to have a scan, too.'

'A scan? Why, there's nothing wrong…?'

'No, as far as I know, everything is fine. But I see from your notes that there's a family history of twins. We just need to be perfectly sure how many babies we're dealing with here.'

Following Cathy Wallace out into the corridor a few minutes later, Holly found herself smiling. She had forgotten that there were pleasures to be found in medicine, as well as the less happy events, and it came as a shock now to realise that she had missed that kind of involvement.

Lost in thought, she turned, only to collide heavily with another figure. She swayed, caught off balance, and instinctively Jamie reached out, grasping her arm to steady her as he straightened up.

'Sorry,' she gasped.

'My pleasure.' Jamie grinned. 'Always here to help a maiden in distress. Not that many come my way, more's the pity.' He gathered up one of the cards she had dropped, placing it in her hands. 'So, how's your first day, then?'

'Fine. At least I don't think I've managed to upset anyone so far, anyway.' She gave a slight smile. 'It's all a bit scary, actually.'

'It's bound to seem a bit strange at first. You'll soon get the hang of it, and the folk around here are generally a good bunch. If it's any consolation, it gets easier. Or that's the theory, anyway.'

Seeing the smile which didn't quite reach the tired brown eyes, Holly shook her head. 'I'd like to feel I'm pulling my weight. That's the reason I'm here after all. Just let me know what the rota is and I'll do my full share.'

'Oh, there's plenty of time for that. As for pulling your weight, I for one am jolly glad to have you here.' He gave a deep-throated chuckle. 'I've been so tired lately I'm sometimes not even sure how I got to the surgery.'

Holly grinned. She couldn't help it. Jamie Nichols's sense of humour was just the light-hearted kind she needed.

'Well, just let me know when you're likely to be on the road so that I can take evasive action, that's all.'

'Finished surgery already?' Callum addressed James crisply as he came along the corridor towards them. 'The waiting room still looks pretty full.'

His glance skated over Holly, his expression cool, and she felt a faint rush of colour invade her cheeks as his gaze took in the classic lines of her straight, knee-length skirt and the bright, cherry-coloured sweater she was wearing.

Jamie removed his hand from her shoulder. 'I'm just away on my rounds,' he said amiably. 'I was on my way to the treatment room to collect something when Holly and I literally bumped into each other.' About to move away, he said as an afterthought, 'Perhaps we can get together some time? I can introduce you to a few people, friends of mine.'

Without turning her head, Holly could sense Callum McLoud's blue eyes watching her. The set of his mouth suggested that he was angry and she found herself wondering why, what she could possibly have done to justify it. Perhaps he didn't approve of relationships between members of the practice.

But surely he couldn't think...? The idea was so ludicrous she almost laughed aloud. On the other hand, a spark of rebellion asserted itself. Just because he was, in effect, her boss, that didn't give him the right to organise her social life as well.

She flashed him a look, before bestowing her nicest smile on Jamie.

'Yes, that sounds nice. I shall look forward to it.'

With a wave of his hand, Jamie went off along the corridor, leaving her alone with Callum.

'I'd suggest that if you must arrange your social calendar, you do it outside working hours in future,' he said coolly.

'I'll be sure to do that,' she said thinly. 'And now, if you'll excuse me, I wouldn't want you to get the idea I wasn't pulling my weight.'

Dismissively she started to walk away, but his hand shot out, capturing her arms and pulling her towards him. His touch had a strange effect on her.

Angry as she was at his unjustified attack, a burning sensation coursed through her, leaving her feeling oddly dazed and breathless. She stared up at him, confused yet again by her reaction to a man she scarcely knew.

The blue eyes returned her gaze steadily and he said softly, 'You really will have to keep your mind on your job, Doctor, otherwise there's no knowing what predicament you might find yourself in.' Then his mouth twisted in a mocking smile and he released her, moving briskly away.

She watched him go, her heart racing illogically. What had she taken on? It was only her first day and already she was wondering how on earth she was going to work with this man. Callum McLoud was provoking and unsettling and she had never met anyone quite like him before.

Over the course of the next few days, Holly managed to settle into a routine and actually found herself beginning to enjoy her work.

A flu epidemic saw patients flocking to the surgery and, with the rapidly falling temperatures as winter got into its stride, she found herself offering advice, mainly to her more elderly patients, on the wisdom of eating sensibly and keeping warm.

Not that the majority needed it. Most of the locals had lived in Glenloch all their lives and were cheerfully hardened to the elements. Even so, there were some, the more frail—especially those who lived alone—who gave her cause for concern.

She walked into Reception, smiling as she unfastened her jacket, and paused briefly to rest her hands on the radiator. 'Oh, that's a relief. Morning, Agnes. Morning, Fiona.'

'Good morning, Doctor, you're nice and early.' Agnes nodded in the direction of the window. 'It's still snowing, I see.' She handed Holly the mail and Holly flicked through it, ruefully already recognising the inevitable promotions informing her of the very latest in drugs and medical care.

'Come away in, Mrs Stevens.' Agnes smiled at the woman who came to the desk. 'Doctor will be with you in about five minutes. Just take a seat.'

Holly shuffled the mail into a pile. 'Yes, well, most of these will have to wait their turn, I'm afraid.' She peered at the list of messages and groaned as, grinning, Fiona handed her a batch of patients' cards.

'All yours, Doctor. There's a nice wee crowd building up out there.'

'You mean I haven't scared them all away?'

The girl chuckled. 'Oh, they're even beginning to ask specially for the new lady doctor.'

'In that case I'd better make a start. Give me a couple of minutes to get myself organised, then send the first one in, will you?'

'Will do.' Fiona waved, and reached for the phone as it began to ring again. 'Yes, Mr Preston. Nurse will see you on Friday, then. Oh, by the way, Doctor,' she said, scribbling an entry into the diary, 'David Galbraith called in, asking if you could see him today.' She consulted the appointments book. 'I told him you're pretty busy.'

Holly frowned. 'Did you ask him if he could make it another day?'

'Aye, but he seemed a wee bit worried...'

'In that case, certainly I'll see him, provided he doesn't

mind waiting. Oh, heavens.' Looking at her watch, she grabbed the bundle of cards and headed for her room.

Shedding her coat, Holly checked her appearance in the mirror before sitting at her desk. Her cheeks were still flushed from the cold wind, adding emphasis to her green eyes, her thick hair was swept back and a touch of lipstick had been applied to her full soft mouth.

Her gaze travelled slowly over the brightly coloured, high-necked sweater and neat, knee-length skirt. Not very fashionable maybe but, then, the meagre contents of her wardrobe had failed miserably under scrutiny. The truth was it had been a long time since she had thought about clothes, especially about buying something new. There hadn't been any reason to do so.

She blinked hard. Why had the thought come rushing in now? After all, nothing had changed—had it? Yes, she was working, but it was only a temporary arrangement, wasn't it? After that…?

Her train of thought was interrupted by a tap at the door as a young woman ushered a fractious four-year-old girl and a runny-nosed toddler into the room.

Holly invited the woman to sit down and the older child promptly eased herself onto her mother's knee, burying her face against the woman's coat, while the toddler proceeded to investigate the contents of the desk, watched by his weary-faced mother who seemed only too pleased to have the pressure diverted, even temporarily, from herself.

'They've both had colds for about a week now, and the pair of them are driving me mad, Doctor. Young Mairie here says her ears hurt, and Ewan is off his food. It's not like him. He's usually such a good eater, but all he wants is juice. Well, he can't live on that, can he?'

Holly retrieved a jar of spatulas from a sticky hand and smiled. 'It won't do him any harm not to eat for a while, Mrs Fraser, as long as he has plenty of fluids. If he prefers flavoured drinks to milk or water, I'd let him have them for a while, provided you avoid the ones with a high sugar content. Let's have a look at you, shall we, young man?'

It didn't really need an examination to tell her that the toddler was suffering from nothing more than an irritating but perfectly normal cold, but she made the usual careful investigations. She checked the child's throat and ears, listening to his chest and feeling his neck for raised glands.

'Well, he's not too bad. There's no sign of a chest infection. His ears are slightly pink but they're not infected. His glands are slightly up, but generally I'd say he's got quite a nasty cold so he's probably feeling grotty, aren't you, poor little chap?'

She ruffled the toddler's hair. 'You can give him Calpol. It will help to keep his temperature down and generally make him feel better.'

Smiling, she turned her attention to the little girl who stared at her with anxious eyes. 'And, Mairie, you've got earache. Reaching for her auroscope, she showed it to the child. 'I just want to shine this light into your ears so that I can see what's making them hurt.'

It took a couple of minutes' persuasion and the promise of a coloured sweetie before she was finally able to make a gentle examination of the child's ears and listen to her chest.

'I'm going to give Mairie an antibiotic, Mrs Fraser.' Holly tapped out a prescription. 'Her chest is clear but she does have quite a nasty ear infection. As I say, this medicine should help. I'm sure you'll see an improvement over the next couple of days. If not, or you're at all worried, please, come back and see me again.'

Jeannie Fraser got to her feet, clutching the prescription with a smile of relief and gathering her children about her. Smiling, Holly saw her out.

All in all it was a busy morning, and it was two hours

later when the door opened slowly and, looking up from the notes she had just completed, Holly watched as her final patient edged his way into the consulting room.

'Hello. It's Mr Galbraith, isn't it?' She smiled. 'I'm sorry you've had rather a long wait. Do come and sit down and tell me what I can do for you.'

Aged sixty-four, David Galbraith was tall and wiry. His face was anxious as he eased himself into the chair. 'It's a bit embarrassing, doctor. I don't want to be a nuisance…'

Holly smiled what she hoped was a reassuring smile. 'You're not being a nuisance, Mr Galbraith. I'm here to help.'

'Aye, well…' The man stared at his hands, seeming uncertain where to begin. 'It's the waterworks, you see. I've been having a spot of bother lately.'

Frowning, Holly scanned the notes. 'I don't seem to have any record…'

'No.' David Galbraith seemed to be having difficulty meeting her gaze. 'Well, it's not an easy sort of thing to talk about, is it? I mean, a man of my age, always on the run, so to speak.'

'When you say "always on the run", how often do you mean?'

'It's got to the point where I'm almost afraid to go anywhere unless I can be sure there are toilets.' He kneaded his hands together anxiously. 'And the damned annoying thing is that when I do go…' He bit at his lower lip and she could see the faint flush in his cheeks.

'You have problems with the flow?'

'Aye, that's it. I don't feel as if I've finished.'

'Do you experience any other kind of discomfort?'

He nodded. 'A sort of burning sensation.'

'Did you bring a urine specimen with you?'

He nodded, producing a small bottle, discreetly wrapped in a brown paper bag, from his pocket.

Taking it from him, Holly was at once struck by the abnormal colour of the specimen, but her expression betrayed nothing of her thoughts as she rose to her feet.

'I'll just test this now. It will only take a few seconds. It's possible you've got a urinary infection.' She carried out the simple test and moved to the wash-basin to wash her hands.

She wished she could still the rising feeling of concern. Drying her hands, she returned to the desk. 'Yes, well, there are signs of an infection.'

'Can you do something about it, then? Some tablets or something?'

'Yes, of course. I can prescribe a course of antibiotics which should help.' She made out a prescription but made no attempt to hand it over. 'This frequent need to spend a penny—is it worse at night?'

David Galbraith gave a slight laugh. 'Aye. It's a damn nuisance, apart from the fact that I keep disturbing the wife. She's not too happy about it. That's one reason why I decided to come and see you.'

'Yes, well, I'm glad you did.' Holly frowned. 'Look, while you're here I'd like to make a quick examination— if that's all right? If you'd just like to slip out of some of your clothes and pop up onto the couch.'

She carried out her examination as gently as possible. 'OK, that's fine, Mr Galbraith. That's all over. You can get dressed now.' Washing her hands at the small basin again, she dried them and returned to sit at her desk.

'How long have you had these symptoms, Mr Galbraith?'

His gaze slid away. 'A while.'

Holly felt her stomach tighten. 'When you say a while, do you mean days? Weeks?'

The man passed his tongue over his lips. 'It's probably been a month or two.'

Holly felt her spirits plummet. 'A month or two, Mr Galbraith?'

He cleared his throat. 'Well, maybe a bit more.' He stared fixedly at his hands now. 'Eight or nine.' He looked up, his eyes suddenly wide in some sort of mute appeal.

'I know I should have come to see someone sooner, but you know how it is. You keep telling yourself it's not important, that it'll go away.' He broke off. 'But it's not gone away. It…it's not good, is it?'

Holly studied him in silence for a moment, then with an effort managed a smile. 'I really think it's too early to draw any conclusions. Any number of conditions could produce the symptoms you describe. It does sound as if you have a bit of a problem with your prostate. The prostate is a small gland at the base of the bladder and in some cases, as men grow older, the gland can become enlarged.'

Panic widened the man's eyes. 'But that can be dangerous, can't it? I've heard about it.'

'Let's not jump to conclusions,' Holly advised softly. 'The important thing is to send you to the hospital for some tests so that we know precisely what we're dealing with.'

'But it *can* be treated?'

'If the prostate is enlarged, surgery may be necessary to remove the gland.'

'And that can cure it?' David Galbraith looked pale and abstracted.

'It can be very successful.' Holly handed over the prescription. 'They'll probably do a number of other tests. You may need an X-ray. In the meantime, I'd like you to take this course of antibiotics to help clear the infection.'

She smiled slightly. 'I'll write to the hospital to make an appointment for you to be seen by a specialist.' She rose to her feet, following as the man made his way to the door. 'Your appointment should come through fairly quickly. Once we have the results we'll take it from there. Meanwhile, if you have any worries or problems, come back to see me.'

The man left and Holly sat back in her chair, feeling suddenly drained. This was the one aspect of her job she had always hated. The feeling of acute helplessness.

No amount of training ever prepared you for the times of frustration and despair when you knew that the odds were stacked against a patient. She had always hoped it would get easier as she became more experienced, but it never had.

She stood up again to replace a book on the shelf, her movements oddly disjointed as she fought the wave of unhappy thoughts that threatened to swamp her. Life could be so cruel, so unfair.

She was scarcely aware of the tapping at the door until it opened and Callum came into the room. He stood in front of her desk, blotting out everything else. She stared at him, resenting the intrusion, her breathing laboured as she fought to bring her emotions under control.

She had forgotten he was off duty until her vision cleared sufficiently for her to take in the fact that he was wearing jeans. He was carrying his leather jacket slung over one shoulder, revealing tautly muscled arms and chest beneath a dark blue sweatshirt.

For a moment she found herself wondering who was going to the lucky recipient of those devastatingly good looks.

She pulled herself up sharply, frowning with concentrated interest at the titles in front of her but seeing nothing.

'Can I do something for you?' she said peevishly.

One dark eyebrow rose. 'I've obviously caught you at a bad moment. I can always come back later.'

What was it about this man, she wondered, that he only had to be near her for her natural calm professionalism to fly out of the window?

Her head rose and she felt the full weight of those blue eyes studying her. 'No.' She cleared her throat. 'It's all right. I'm sorry, I just have a bit of a headache, that's all.' And suddenly her heart wasn't feeling too steady either! 'What can I do for you?'

He stood with his hands in his pockets. 'It occurred to me that you may not know that Jamie is due for one of those obligatory study days next week. I didn't want you to worry about cover. I'll double up on surgery. It's only once in a while.'

'Oh—right.' Without even being aware of it, her fingers rearranged the items on her desk. 'Well, thanks for letting me know, but I'll be quite happy to do an extra duty if necessary.'

Callum studied her, a frown drawing his dark brows together. He dropped his jacket onto a chair. 'Holly, what's wrong?'

She moistened her lips, wishing there was some way she could avoid his shrewd gaze, but his hands caught at her arms and turned her to face him when she would have moved away.

His touch sent tiny shock waves darting through her. She drew a deep breath, her face taut with strain. 'I don't know what you mean.'

His gaze narrowed. 'You're not a very good liar. Something must have happened.' His frown deepened. 'Has someone upset you?'

She stared at him with her jaw clenched, her mouth making a grim, hard line. Callum watched her, waiting.

'Go on,' he persisted.

She stiffened, trying to pull away. 'If you really want to know, I'm angry.' She shook her head. 'Maybe angry's not the right word. Upset. I don't know—' She broke off, raking a hand through her hair.

'I take it this has to do with the patient I just saw leaving?'

'David Galbraith. You know him?'

'Galbraith. Yes, I think so, though not particularly well. He was one of Alex's patients.' He frowned. 'Married. Two grown-up children, couple of grandchildren. What's the problem?'

She sighed heavily. 'I hope I'm wrong but I think he's showing all the symptoms of advanced prostate cancer.'

'Hell!' Callum's face darkened. 'But you can't be sure. Besides, if it's caught in the early stages…'

'You think I don't know that?' She looked at him. 'Unfortunately, it seems he's had the symptoms for months and has done nothing about it, and now it's probably too late. He's sixty-four years old. Sixty-four! It's no age at all.' Her jaw clenched. 'I feel utterly useless.'

'Hey, come on. It's not your fault. It happens every day, Holly.'

'Oh, and I'm a doctor so I'm supposed to be able to deal with it—is that what you're saying?' Holly stared at him, breathing hard. 'Don't you ever get angry?'

'Yes, of course I do. But if I let myself become emotionally involved I couldn't do the job.' He frowned. 'We're doctors. That doesn't mean we can perform miracles. We can't force a patient to come and see us. David Galbraith is an adult, responsible for his own actions.'

For a moment Holly stared at him in stunned silence. 'So you're saying that makes it all right.'

'No, it doesn't make it all right.' Callum was watching her. 'I just don't see why you're blaming yourself. You didn't cause his condition. I take it you'll be ordering all the necessary tests?'

'Yes, of course I will. But you and I both know it's only

a formality when something is so far advanced. I'm going through the motions, that's all.'

'It's your job,' he said evenly. 'We do the best we can, Holly. Sometimes it's not enough, but our knowledge is growing all the time.'

'It's not going to help David Galbraith, though, is it?' she bit out.

'Maybe not. But he made his own choices. The best we can hope for is that someone else may learn from his mistake. Besides, medicine has progressed, Holly. He stands a far better chance today than he might have done even a few years ago.'

Holly gave a sigh of exasperation then smiled wryly. 'I know you're only trying to make me feel better but somehow it doesn't work. If I'm right, can you imagine what that man is going to go through? What his family—'

'You don't need to tell me what the Galbraiths will have to go through, Holly,' he said quietly. 'My grandfather had prostate cancer. Maybe that's one reason I decided to go into medicine. I had this naïve idea that I could save the world or, if not all of it, at least those people I cared about. It took me a while to realise it was just that—naïve.'

He looked at her and said softly, 'It doesn't work, Holly. You still need to learn that.'

'David Galbraith isn't old,' she bit out. 'He should have a lot more years ahead of him but because of fear…or maybe ignorance, or both, he's probably going to die. What does that say about us and our glorious profession, Doctor? What kind of progress is that?'

'Hey, come on. You can't afford to let your personal anxiety colour your attitude to your work—none of us can. But that doesn't mean we don't have feelings.' His mouth twisted. 'You need to unwind a little, relax more. You have to learn to leave it all behind when you walk out of that door.'

'I'm fine.'

'No, you're not.' Callum frowned. 'I'm not saying the patients aren't important, Holly, but you need to be able to switch off—we all do. Look, I have an idea. Why don't we go out for a meal one evening? Glenloch does actually boast a decent hotel. A change of scene might do you the world of good. How about tomorrow? I could pick you up around eight.'

She looked at him, all too conscious of his nearness. Her mouth felt dry with a nervousness that seemed to have no logic to it. Everything was happening too fast. She wasn't ready for this. She suddenly seemed to be getting out of her depth.

She darted him a glance. 'It's very kind of you, and it's a nice idea, but...well, the truth is, I don't feel ready for dating just yet. I haven't had much of a social life recently.'

'All the more reason to give it a try.' His brows drew together. 'I'm only suggesting a meal, Holly. No strings, just a quiet evening. A chance to relax.'

A quiet evening, alone with him. Relaxing! Somehow the two things didn't seem to equate. Holly's heart gave an extra thud and she said slowly, 'I really think it would be better if we kept things between us on a strictly professional footing. That way we both know where we stand. I hope that doesn't offend you. I...I'd like us to be friends, if you think that's possible.'

His eyes were cool, narrowed on her.

'You really want to know what I think, Dr Hunter?' he said in a low, throaty tone. 'I think you're a coward. A coward. That's what you are.'

CHAPTER FIVE

CALLUM'S words rankled over the following days. She wasn't a coward, Holly told herself repeatedly. Cautious maybe but, then, what was wrong with that? If you'd been hurt badly once, you didn't go out looking for trouble, did you?

Not that one date with Callum McLoud would have led to anything, of course. Maybe she had let her imagination run away with her. The thought set her heart thudding just a shade too quickly for comfort.

Her mind veered sharply away as she parked her car, climbing out just in time to see Callum driving out of the car park.

As he drew level he brought the vehicle to a halt, winding down the window.

'I'm just on my way out, but I thought you'd like to know that I've arranged for a batch of information leaflets to be delivered to the surgery. They should cover most of the subjects our patients are likely to come up against. Heart disease, diabetes and prostate cancer.'

Flakes of snow settled in his hair. 'The display rack should be here in about a week's time.'

She swallowed hard, moved by the realisation that he had actually listened to her fears. 'Oh, that's wonderful.' Her breath formed white clouds in the cold air. 'I'm sure the patients will appreciate it, and if they do have any worries at least they might feel more able to approach us for help.'

He nodded. 'I hope you're right and that patients will make use of the information. By the way, how's Mac?'

'Fine. He's settled in nicely.'

'Good, I'm glad to hear it.'

His eyes were impersonal, his tone purely businesslike. But, then, that was what she wanted. It was for the best, Holly told herself briskly as she watched him drive away. Which didn't quite explain why a small black cloud, which she vaguely recognised as depression, suddenly seemed to be sitting just above her head.

She slammed the car door with unnecessary vigour and began to walk briskly towards the surgery. Cowardice had nothing to do with it. She simply wasn't taking any chances, that was all.

Experience had taught her to be wary. Callum McLoud was an unsettling influence. One she could well do without. She preferred her life the way it was, thank you very much—quiet, maybe even vaguely boring, but uncomplicated and definitely safe.

Holly drew herself up as she walked wearily into Reception where she checked her schedule for the morning. For once, surprisingly, things seemed relatively quiet.

'What happened?' she said, nodding in the direction of the unusually quiet waiting room. 'Was it something I said?'

Fiona grinned. 'Kids back at school, market day, hopefully the end of the flu epidemic.'

'Ah.' Suppressing a yawn, Holly scanned her list of patients.

'Morning.' Jamie deposited his briefcase on the floor, chafing his hands as he peered across the desk at the morning's list. 'None for me? Right, that's me away home, then. Feet up by the fire.'

Fiona chuckled. 'You should be so lucky. Here.' She handed him a pile of cards.

'Damn! Foiled again.' He grinned at Holly. 'How are you settling in?'

'Fine, thanks.' She smiled. 'It's less nerve-racking now that I'm beginning to understand the system.'

'System?' Jamie raised one eyebrow to glance at Agnes Ferguson as she walked into the small office. 'What's all this about a system? No one told me.'

'Och, away with you,' Agnes chided good-humouredly. 'Speak for yourself, Dr Nichols. The rest of us are doing just fine, which is more than can be said for some.' She glanced pointedly at the clock. 'I take it you'll be making a start fairly soon?'

'You're a hard woman, Agnes Ferguson.'

'Aye, so I've been told. So you'll not be wanting coffee later, then, Doctor?'

Jamie gave an exaggerated sigh as he headed for the door, holding it open for Holly. 'It's threats now.'

Holly laughed. 'You're impossible. I don't know why they put up with you.'

'I know.' He grinned. 'But lovely with it.' It was his parting shot before he disappeared into his consulting room.

In her own room, Holly dropped the bundle of files onto her desk and drew a deep breath, before shedding her coat and going to check her appearance in the mirror—fashionable knee-length skirt, vivid bronze-coloured silk shirt.

Seating herself at the desk, she hitched her skirt into place and pressed the bell to summon her first patient of the day.

In fact, it turned out to be a surprisingly busy morning, with the usual batch of sore throats, coughs and backaches. An hour and a half later she was beginning to look forward to her own coffee-break.

'Mrs McLean.' Holly looked up, smiling, as her last patient came hesitantly into the consulting room. 'Sit down and tell me what I can do for you.'

Alice McLean, according to her notes, was sixty-five.

She was thin, her face was pale and she moved awkwardly to sit in the chair.

'I'd just like a repeat of the usual prescription for the rheumatics, if you please, Doctor.'

Holly glanced, frowning, at the computer screen. 'Yes, I gather you've seen Dr Douglas several times about the pain in your joints?'

'Aye, that's right.' Alice McLean gently kneaded the swollen arthritic fingers of her left hand. 'It's been awful painful of late.'

'Yes, I'm sure it must be.' Smiling sympathetically, Holly moved to gently examine the woman's wrists, noting the redness of the inflamed joints. Alice McLean winced slightly and Holly frowned. 'What other joints are affected?'

'My shoulders, and my feet.'

Nodding, Holly returned to sit at her desk where she reread the notes, recognising the name of a well-known drug which she knew to be extremely beneficial in cases such as Alice McLean's. 'I see you had the latest course of painkillers about a month ago.'

The woman shivered, hugging her coat round her as she seemed to struggle to concentrate. Her speech was slow and hesitant. 'Aye, I suppose that would be about right.'

'Do you find the tablets help?'

Alice McLean took time to consider. Finally she shook her head. 'Not so much.'

She seemed short of breath, Holly noticed as, frowning, she reached out and instinctively took the woman's pulse. Somewhere in her head tiny alarm bells were beginning to ring.

What should have been a straightforward case of rheumatoid arthritis didn't seem to be running quite true to form. Alice McLean seemed confused, her pulse rate was racing at a hundred and she was shivering violently, despite the fact that the consulting room was centrally heated.

Holly sat back and watched as the woman picked up her handbag, opened it with trembling hands and proceeded to hunt through it, before closing it again.

'It's not very warm today, is it, Mrs McLean?'

Alice frowned, glancing uncertainly at the window where a thin flurry of snow drifted against the glass. 'No, I suppose it's not.'

Holly smiled. 'I prefer the summer myself. I like to be warm, don't you?'

'Oh, I never feel warm. Come rain or shine, winter or summer, I feel the cold something awful.'

The sound of the alarm bells was suddenly upped a decibel. Holly rose to her feet. 'I'd like to take a look at your neck, Alice. I promise I won't hurt you.'

She made a gentle examination of the woman's neck, concentrating on the area next to the windpipe. 'Do you ever have pain in your ears or jaw, Alice?'

'The woman nodded, her face anxious.

'And have you lost any weight recently?'

'My husband says I'm nothing but a bag of bones. Will I be able to have my tablets, Doctor?'

Holly returned to her seat. 'Yes, of course you will, Alice. But I'd like to try you with some different tablets as well.'

The woman's eyes widened. 'Different?'

'Alice, you must have noticed that you haven't been feeling too well lately. You feel the cold, and you may find that you're a little forgetful, too?'

The woman laughed slightly, but Holly was quick to notice that her eyes had filled with tears.

'Aye, Robert reckons I'm going daft in my old age.'

Holly felt her hackles rise. Gently she placed her hand over the woman's fingers. 'You're not going daft, Alice.'

She frowned. 'Look, I shall need to arrange for you to have some tests.' She saw the look of anxiety on Alice McLean's face. 'Now, don't worry. I think your problem—all your symptoms—may point to a thyroid deficiency.'

'No! Well, I never. My mother had problems with her thyroid, too.'

'Well, that's more than likely.' Holly smiled. 'These things can run in families.'

'But will I be needing an operation?'

Holly shook her head. 'It's highly unlikely. I'll need to take a blood sample from you. I'll send that off to the hospital and, hopefully, they should be able to confirm the diagnosis.'

She reached for her notepad. 'What I'd like you to do is make an appointment to come and see me again in a week's time. The results of the tests should be through by then and we can get you started on a course of replacement therapy.'

'And that's it?'

'Well, not quite.' Holly smiled. 'I shall need to see you at regular intervals, just to be sure the medication suits you and is doing what it's supposed to do. We need to start you on a tiny dose and build it up, otherwise it would make you feel awful. But, apart from that, well, yes, hopefully, that's it.'

She rose to her feet to see the woman out, and Alice McLean left, smiling. Easing her aching muscles, Holly tidied her desk and, minutes later, walked through to Reception.

She deposited the bundle of patients' cards and a folder of letters and forms on the desk in front of Fiona. 'My contribution, I'm afraid.' She smiled at Jamie who was signing letters while at the same time ruefully scanning his list of visits.

'I see now why surgery wasn't so busy. They've all decided to stay home and let me call on them.'

'It's the way you charm them.' Chuckling, Fiona slapped another page in front of him. 'Sign at the bottom, please.'

He groaned. 'How many more? I'm sure I didn't write all these letters.'

Agnes peered round the door of the adjoining office, cocking her head meaningfully in Jamie's direction. 'Some folk are under the impression that dealing with paperwork means filing it in the nearest waste-paper bin.'

Fiona pulled a wry face, reaching out her hand as the phone began to ring again. 'Glenloch Surgery.'

'A defenceless man doesn't stand a chance around here,' Jamie grumbled good-humouredly.

'Yes, the doctor is still here.' Fiona tucked the receiver under her chin as she hunted for a pen, shifting papers and files. 'Yes.' Her face became serious. 'Do you know how many—? Three. What about the ambulance?' She glanced at the clock. 'Yes, the doctor is here with me now.'

Holly said, 'What's the problem?'

'It's Constable Adams. There's been an accident, down by the coast road.'

Holly was aware of the sudden dryness in her mouth, but her response was instantly totally professional as she took the phone. 'Dr Hunter speaking. Give me what details you have, Constable.'

'It's a collision, Doctor. A nasty one. Two cars, several injuries. We can't be more specific at this stage. We're getting a couple of them out now, but one of the drivers looks pretty bad.'

'Oh, no! You've called the emergency services?'

'Aye, but they've a way to come, and the weather's not so good. They may take a while.'

'I'll be with you as fast as I can.' Holly replaced the phone, automatically reaching for her briefcase and jacket.

Jamie glanced up, his face anxious. 'I'll take it if you like.'

For a second she was almost tempted, but she shook her head. 'No, it's all right. You still have patients to see and, besides, I'm on call. Look, I'd better go. I'll see you later.'

It was snowing heavily by the time she reached the scene of the accident. An ambulance was parked close by, its blue lights flashing, its rear doors open. The fire brigade were also in attendance.

Grabbing her briefcase, Holly hurried towards the police officer.

'Constable Adams? You called the surgery. I'm Dr Hunter.'

'Glad to see you, Doctor. I'm afraid it's all a bit of a mess.' The young man led her towards the vehicles. 'As far as we can judge, one car took the bend too fast and hit the car coming in the opposite direction.'

He paused to let a stretcher past. 'We've managed to get one of the drivers out. He's on his way to hospital. The passenger is being removed from the wreckage now, but we're having a problem with the other driver. As far as we can tell, he's trapped.'

Holly's horrified gaze took in the crumpled wreckage of a small car. It seemed to be partially wedged beneath the larger vehicle. She felt her stomach muscles contract.

'My God, what sort of state is the driver in?'

'He's alive, or at least he was. One of the ambulance chaps managed to reach him and said there was a pulse. Trouble is, the door is jammed. The fire officers are having to cut through the roof to get him out.'

Holly drew a deep breath. 'I'd better take a look.'

The next half-hour went by in a blur. She tended the

passenger from the first car, splinting a fractured arm and stemming bleeding from a head wound—working quickly.

There was scarcely time to breathe a sigh of relief as he was driven away in the waiting ambulance before the second driver was stretchered over to her.

'He's in a pretty bad way, Doc.' One of the ambulance men knelt beside her.

Even in the dull, grey afternoon light, she could see that the victim's lips were a bluish grey and when she checked his eyes she found that the pupils were enlarged. Her fingers went quickly to his neck.

'There's no pulse,' she said to the paramedic. 'He's stopped breathing. I'll do mouth-to-mouth, you try compression.'

They worked in unison, the paramedic pushing down on the man's breastbone several times while she tilted the man's head back, lifted his chin and then, pinching his nose, breathed into his mouth twice.

She waited while the paramedic applied compression again. For the first time she looked properly at the victim. He was young, she guessed around twenty-four. Her stomach tightened. Suddenly she felt sick. It could have been Tony lying there, so pale, lifeless.

Her fingers shook as she checked again for a pulse. 'Nothing. Keep trying.'

'I don't think it's going to work, Doc. I reckon he's gone.'

'We can't just give up. He can't just die.' Angrily she pushed the man aside and began the compressions herself, pausing to breathe into the victim's mouth again.

After a few moments she stopped. She stared down at the lifeless form and felt her throat tighten. 'He can't die. he can't. He's too young. It isn't fair.'

The paramedic put his arm round her shoulders. 'Come on, Doc. You've done all you could. He was dead before we got him out.' Gently he drew her to her feet. 'He didn't stand a chance, but at least we tried.'

But it hadn't been enough, had it? She clung weakly to his arm. Despite the fact that it was snowing and the temperature was heading rapidly for zero, her skin felt hot and clammy.

'It's such a waste.' Her voice seemed to be stuck somewhere in her throat.

'It always is.' The paramedic looked at her, his expression grim. 'Whatever their age, this job never gets any easier. You do what you can. Will you be all right?'

Holly nodded, brushing a tangle of hair from her temple. She was hardly aware of walking back to her car or driving to the surgery.

It as a relief to find it empty and quiet. Evening surgery wasn't due to start for another hour so she walked through the waiting room and along the corridor to her own room.

Pushing open the door, she put her briefcase down and wearily dropped her jacket onto the chair. She was surprised to find that her hands were shaking.

After two years Holly had imagined she was beginning to get her feelings under control, but the accident, the futility of it all, the terrible waste of a young life, had brought it all flooding back.

She stood at the window, staring out but seeing nothing. How long did it take, she wondered, to get over something like that—the feelings of helplessness? Or maybe you never did. The thought was almost unbearable.

Pressing a hand to her head, she closed her eyes in an attempt to shut out memories that still had the power to haunt her.

She didn't even hear the door open—wasn't aware of the tall figure standing there—until he closed the door quietly.

She whirled round.

Callum glanced at her strained expression. 'What's happened?'

She drew a shaky breath, feeling a sudden wave of exhaustion hit her again. 'Nothing. I'll be fine.' And then, as he moved towards her, she warded him off, putting her arms around her own body in a self-protective embrace.

'Really, I'm fine.' Her voice rose slightly, a betraying tremor in the words. 'Why should anything be wrong?'

Callum frowned as his hands shifted to curve around her shoulders, forcing her to look at him. 'I'm not blind, Holly. Besides, you have a very expressive face. Whatever it is, tell me. Talk about it. Was it the accident? Jamie told me you'd been called out.'

'You don't need to worry.' Her voice was taut, her fingers twisting relentlessly. 'I won't go to pieces. I'm still perfectly capable of doing my job.'

'I didn't suggest otherwise.' His jaw was hard, controlled, only a flicker of muscle giving any sign of his own inner tension. 'I'm not worried about the practice, Holly. I'm worried about you.'

She drew a shaky breath, knowing that she wasn't being fair to him. 'It was an RTA. One of the victims died and I let it get to me, that's all.'

She swallowed hard on the tightness in her throat. 'He was so young. It was all such a bloody waste. Like I said, I let it get to me. It isn't your problem,' she managed fretfully. 'I'll deal with it. There's no need for you to be involved.'

Callum's dark brows drew together. 'Holly, don't you know me better than that?'

She tried to pull away from him, wanting to be alone, to think, to rebuild her crumpled defences. But he didn't let her go. Instead, he drew her towards him.

His dark, expensively tailored jacket brushed softly against her skin, sending dangerous and totally illogical signals to her brain. For a moment she resisted, then, sighing, she relaxed wearily against him.

'I'm sorry.'

'Don't be,' he rasped. 'There's nothing wrong with caring, Holly. We're doctors—that doesn't mean we're not allowed to care.'

'I thought you said we shouldn't become emotionally involved.'

'It's different. We're human beings, with emotions, like everyone else. We can't just switch them off.' His thumb grazed the softness of her cheek.

'*I'm* human too, Holly. Don't shut me out. You don't have a monopoly on feelings. I care, too. Maybe it's time you realised that. Emotions aren't a sign of weakness.'

He sounded quietly angry. The words were forced out in a roughened undertone and, hearing it, she looked up at him, her eyes widening as they focussed with renewed clarity on the tautly honed features, on the firmly moulded mouth that hovered just inches above her own.

She was held firmly within the circle of his arms, her soft curves crushed against his hard frame so that she could almost feel the tension vibrating within his long, muscled body.

Holly was shaken by the riot of emotions that coursed through her. 'I'm sorry,' she said shakily again. 'I thought I was over the accident. What happened today… It brought everything back.'

'Tony?'

She nodded bleakly. 'The man who died… He was so young. He had everything to live for.'

'I know,' he said softly. 'It never gets easier, but you don't have to cope alone.'

'It isn't that easy. These last two years I've learned to be self-sufficient. I've had to be. I don't know that I can be any other way.'

Callum looked down at her. A muscle pulsed in his jaw. 'You have to learn to let go, Holly,' he urged softly. 'There's no going back. You can't change anything. There's a whole new world out there, a whole new future, waiting. You just have to want it.'

The husky tones lapped at the edges of her resistance. She felt the breath catch in her throat as he cupped her face, bringing her so close that her nostrils were invaded by the familiar smell of him.

Shock briefly widened her eyes at the realisation that he was going to kiss her—and it hazily registered on her shell-shocked mind that she wanted him to. The sensuous mouth was just a breath away.

'It's a question of trust, Holly. Just let go.'

She stood, stunned by the power of the sensations that coursed through her. Her limbs felt strangely weak and she clung to him. Her fingers curved, tensing over his wide shoulders, taking the strength they offered.

She should stop this now, an inner voice warned, before it was too late. She felt his gaze sweep over the creamy translucence of her skin and she began to tremble as he lifted his head and for a moment looked into her face. Then she was lost to all thought as his mouth closed on hers and began to explore the softness of her lips with a warm and tender possession that was unexpectedly sweet.

This shouldn't be happening, she told herself. She made a tiny sound of protest, trying to turn her head away, but he wouldn't allow it and pulled her closer still, if that were possible.

'What are you so afraid of, Holly?' Callum rasped. 'You must know I'd never hurt you.'

Not intentionally, maybe. The thought hovered. Then she was lost to all reason as the kiss deepened in intensity. Her body seemed to have no will of its own.

The depth of her response shocked her. She had never

known such instant, mind-shattering awareness as this and it brought a shimmer of confusion to her eyes, made her stare up at him in uncertain dismay.

His own eyes reflected the turmoil that was going on inside her. Tension sparked in the blue depths, a glittering, febrile emotion flickering there, and she saw it, recognised it for what it was. Desire. Nothing more, nothing less.

Moaning softly, she swayed in his arms. He had started off with good intentions, she was sure, offering her comfort, and she had been weak enough to accept it, grateful for his strength. She had no one to blame but herself for what had happened next.

She made a last, belated effort to draw away, a new and unaccustomed ache growing inside her.

'Holly,' he groaned softly as his mouth made feathery advances over her throat, chin, lips, eyes and back to her mouth, claiming it with a fierceness that left them both breathless.

She responded with a ferocity that matched his own, measure for measure. His mouth left hers as he stroked her hair.

'Have you any idea how much I want you?' he choked. 'I need you, Holly.'

She raised herself to reach his mouth. 'I know—' She broke off with another moan as he kissed her again. Then she felt him tense and wanted to weep as he set her free. His breathing was harsh as he drew away and she became dizzyingly aware of the open door.

'Ah, Doctor.' Fiona's voice intruded cheerfully into the tension like a thunderclap. 'I was hoping I'd catch you before you start surgery. Those reports you've been waiting for on Mr McGwerter have come through at last.'

Callum's facial muscles flickered spasmodically, his mouth making a grim line, and Holly struggled to find her own voice.

'Yes, well, I'll leave you to it, then,' she managed, heading for the door. 'I've another call to make.'

'Holly, wait. We have to talk.'

She fled, ignoring his appeal. Gasping as a gust of icy wind hit her, she climbed into the car, grated the gears and swore under breath, all too aware of the figure reflected in her driving mirror as she drove away.

Holly felt confused and unsettled, dazed by her reaction to a man she scarcely knew, incapable of understanding fully the tumult of sensations she had experienced in Callum's arms. Pleasure, confusion—all the things which led up to the kind of emotional battering she had promised herself she would never feel again.

Suddenly she was grateful that the interruption had come when it had, before it was too late. Things were happening too fast, moving beyond her control. She was beginning to like Callum McLoud, perhaps a little too much for her own well-being, and she ought to have known better than to let her feelings run away with her.

He was just a man, she reminded herself firmly. All right, an *attractive* man who, with typical male arrogance, had made a play for her. But that was all there was to it. She had been vulnerable and he had had no hesitation in taking advantage of the fact.

She ought to have learned her lesson by now. She had spent the past eighteen months trying to get her life back together. She wasn't going to see it all ruined now.

It was dark when a couple of hours later Holly heard Callum's car draw up outside the cottage. She sat in the dark with Mac at her feet, gazing into the fire as she ate chocolate biscuits. Comfort food.

Mac lifted his head, a warning rumble in his throat as he glanced at the door. She heard Callum's footsteps on the gravel outside, and tensed as they paused and he knocked at the door.

'Holly! I know you're in there. At least let's talk.'

But it wouldn't be 'at least', would it? It would become more. It would start with talk and then he would kiss her and— But she wasn't going to think about that and she was definitely not going to answer the door.

An hour later she had managed to eat some real food and had finally fallen into bed, determined to have an early night, only to find, frustratingly, that sleep eluded her.

Lying awake and staring up at the ceiling, she found her thoughts drifting restlessly back to the events of the day and her response to Callum's kiss. Emotion suddenly tightened her throat at the growing realisation that, like it or not, he had become an important factor in her life.

Defensively she plumped her pillows and buried her head beneath the blankets. It had taken two years to build a protective shell around herself after Tony had died. She had thought she had succeeded until now.

She sat up, plumping her pillows crossly again with her fist. But not firmly enough to blot the image of Callum McLoud from her thoughts completely. Blast the man! Why had he come walking into her life, filling it with complications? He had no right at all.

It was a question of trust, he had said. But right now she wasn't sure she could trust herself, let alone him!

CHAPTER SIX

GETTING up out of a warm bed in the middle of the night, especially on a freezing winter one, definitely didn't get any easier, Holly decided.

She could hear the ice crunching beneath her feet as she made her way carefully to her car, her breath white in the air as she hunted for her keys and scraped the windscreen, wryly acknowledging that this was one aspect of the job she had never got used to. And why was it always on the coldest, darkest night?

Not that she had been asleep. Shuffling her feet on the frozen ground, she juggled her keys and finally managed to unlock the car door.

She had tried putting her restlessness down to the cheese on toast she'd had for supper, having felt too tired to cook a proper meal, but knew it had far more to do with a kiss.

For the past few days, whenever their paths had crossed, Callum had treated her with nothing more than cool formality and, perversely, she felt cheated. She had thought it was what she wanted, but now she wasn't so sure. She felt bewildered by the conflicting emotions his behaviour stirred in her.

It was some small consolation that at least they managed to work together without allowing the tensions to show.

Stifling a yawn, Holly brought the car to a halt outside the McGiver's house some ten minutes later, and reached for her briefcase. The door opened as she manoeuvred her way cautiously along the path.

'Oh, Doctor, come away in.' Seventy-year-old Gordon McGiver ushered her into the house. He looked anxious and pale. 'Joan's in the kitchen on the floor. I didn't know whether I should try to move her.'

'You did the right thing, leaving her where she is.' Holly was quick to offer the reassurance as she followed the man into the warm kitchen where his wife lay on her side on the well-scrubbed floor.

Putting down her briefcase, Holly quickly tugged off her gloves and knelt beside the unconscious woman.

Gordon McGiver gazed anxiously down at his wife. 'I didn't know what to do for the best, but I'd seen a programme on TV about what to do in an emergency.'

'I couldn't have done better myself, Mr McGiver.' Holly looked up at him and smiled slightly. The woman was lying in the lateral position, on her left side, with the upper arm and leg pointing forward. 'There's always a risk that an unconscious person might vomit and choke if they're left lying on their back.'

As she spoke she was carrying out a quick but gentle examination. Joan McGiver's limbs were slightly spastic and her neck was totally rigid, a classic sign, Holly recognised with growing concern, of irritation of the brain.

'You said on the phone that your wife had complained of a headache before she collapsed.'

'Aye, that's right. She was a wee bit restless and got up to make a cup of tea. I was awake anyway, so I followed her down. She was standing over there.'

Gordon McGiver pointed to the kitchen sink. 'She'd filled the kettle and was just standing there. Suddenly she looked at me and said, ''Gordon, something just hit me at the back of my head.'' Well, I knew there was nothing. Then she just fell down.' Tears filled the man's eyes as he looked at Holly. 'It's not good, is it, Doctor?'

'I'm afraid it isn't, Gordon, though at this stage it's impossible to tell how bad it is.'

A shuddering sigh escaped the man's lips. 'Is it her heart? There's been no sign…'

'No, I don't think so.' Holly was already reaching for her mobile phone. 'I think it's possible your wife may have had a subarachnoid haemorrhage, Mr McGiver.' She saw him shake his head. 'You can see that her neck is totally rigid. That's a classic sign of irritation of the surface of the brain.'

She rose to her feet, already tapping out a number on the phone. 'I'm going to arrange to get her into hospital.'

'I want to go with her.'

'Yes, of course, that's not a problem,' Holly said gently. 'Though you realise she may be there for some time?'

As she replaced the phone in her pocket moments later, she breathed an inward sigh of relief. At least help was on the way, but it was still going to be a long struggle for Joan McGiver.

'Do you have any relatives close by?' she said. 'Someone who can stay with you for a while, perhaps bring you home later?'

'Aye.' The man's face clouded with confusion. 'There's my son…'

'Why not give him a call? Or would you like me to do it for you?'

'No, it's best coming from me.'

Holly nodded.

'What will they do to her, Doctor?'

'They'll want to do a lumbar puncture first to confirm the diagnosis.'

'And will they want to operate?'

'It's possible,' Holly said gently. 'I really can't say for sure.' There was nothing to be gained by telling the man his wife may not even survive the next few hours. She had to be positive. 'That will be up to the neurosurgeon. For now the important thing is to get her into hospital where she'll get the care she needs.'

It was another half-hour before she drove back to the cottage where she showered and made herself a hot drink, before finally falling into bed. Exhausted, she pulled the blankets around her and closed her eyes.

She woke to bright daylight with a splitting headache, and to the horrifying realisation that she had overslept.

Maybe because she had had her mind on other things, or simply because she had been tired—whatever the reason—she had somehow forgotten to reset the alarm. Consequently she arrived at the surgery breathless and having had no breakfast, as well as being ten minutes late.

Nor did it help matters, when she paused at the desk to gather up her lists of visits for the morning, to find Callum already there, grimly contemplating his morning surgery list.

His glance skimmed over her as she walked into the small office, his expression darkly frowning.

'Good morning,' she said, juggling her briefcase and a bundle of mail.

'Is it?' The laconic tone made her pause as she hunted for her hopefully temporarily mislaid mobile phone.

Frowning, she closed the locks on her briefcase before she looked up at him. 'Well, I'm at least hoping it won't get any worse,' she murmured, wondering what had brought on his black mood and deciding to ignore it. 'I hadn't *planned* to be late,' she said pithily. 'I was called out in the early hours of the morning—'

'I know,' he said evenly. 'I heard you drive past the cottage around four-thirty.'

She stiffened, sensing a reproach. 'I'm very sorry, Doctor. I'll do my best not to disturb you in future.'

A nerve pulsed in his jaw and Holly felt an unexpected

tremor run through her as he looked down at her with brooding eyes.

'It does seem to be becoming something of a habit, doesn't it?' he remarked, a cool grimace twisting his mouth.

Was he being funny? She glared intently at the attractive planes of his face, looking for some sign of amusement at her expense. His mouth was nerve-shatteringly sensual.

She drew herself up sharply. 'It was almost dawn before I fell into bed again. I'm beginning to think it was a mistake—falling asleep again. I feel worse than if I'd stayed awake.'

'So, what was the emergency?'

She ran a hand wearily through her hair. 'Gordon McGiver called. His wife had collapsed. He was obviously worried sick.'

Callum frowned. '*Joan* McGiver?'

'Yes, that's right.'

'I didn't know she'd been ill recently.'

'She hadn't.' Thrusting a hand absently into her jacket pocket, she found the mobile phone, and with a sigh of relief dropped it into her briefcase. 'It all happened very suddenly.'

His gaze narrowed. 'When you say "collapsed", what do you mean exactly?'

Holly looked at him sharply. Was he actually questioning her judgement? 'I mean just that. One minute she was apparently standing at the kitchen sink. She complained of feeling as if something had hit her at the back of the head, then she collapsed.'

She frowned. 'I hate to say it but it sounds to me like a classic case of subarachnoid haemorrhage.' Her mouth twisted in annoyance. 'Look, I don't know why I'm bothering to explain all this. All right, so I was a few minutes late but I'll make up the time. It's hardly my fault if you're having a bad morning.'

She saw the muscle tighten in his jaw and wondered again what had brought on his unaccustomed mood. It couldn't be anything she had done—or had failed to do—surely?

His own glance moved glitteringly over her, making a swift assessment of the soft, red, roll-neck sweater which clung gently to her feminine curves, and dropping to sweep over the neatly tailored trousers which emphasised the slender curve of her waist and hips. She had dressed in a hurry, for warmth and practicality, but under that raking glance she felt her colour beginning to rise.

Crisply, she said, 'Do you usually take your moods out on everyone else?'

He frowned. 'I wasn't aware that was what I was doing.'

'Maybe no one wants to risk getting their head bitten off for telling you.' Returning his stare, her gaze ran the length of him, taking in the clean lines of his expensively tailored suit. His dark, casually styled hair looked as if it had been recently trimmed.

She had to resist an almost compulsive yet totally illogical desire to run her fingers through its silky darkness and disturb its neatness.

She swallowed hard. 'Yes, well, it's late. I'd better make a start.' She walked through the small office to collect a pack of sterile gloves from the supply cupboard.

'Holly, wait.'

Callum followed her, pausing in the doorway. 'You're right, I'm sorry. I'm not having a good day so far.' His mouth made a wry curve. 'I hadn't even taken my jacket off when a rep turned up without an appointment, expecting to be seen before surgery. He said he only wanted a brief chat. He wasted half an hour. I wasn't happy, I can tell you.'

Holly could believe it, and she almost found it in herself to feel sympathy for the man. 'I dare say you made your feelings clear,' she said with a wry half-smile.

'Oh I think he got the message. I told him either he makes a proper appointment in future or he waits at the end of the queue. I'm certainly not about to start prescribing drugs I know nothing about, and I'm not likely to be won over by a heated discussion on them at eight in the morning before I've had at least one cup of coffee.'

Holly gave a slight smile. 'I think we can safely take it that his day didn't start too well either.' Her glance went to the coffee percolator on a small side table, and she put her briefcase down.

'Look, we both seem to have started off on the wrong foot. I don't know about you, but I could certainly do with a cup before I start. I'm not at my best until I've built up a decent caffeine level.'

Frowning, he looked at his watch. 'Sounds like a great idea.'

She poured two cups of coffee while he skimmed through the case notes he was holding.

'Sugar?'

He nodded absently and she queried softly, 'Is there a problem?'

He dropped the cards on to the table as she proffered a cup. 'Problem? I'm not sure yet. It could be.'

'Can you tell me?' She watched as he stirred the coffee.

'It's a child. A five-year-old. The family moved to this area about six months ago.' He stirred his coffee, gazing into the dark, steaming liquid. 'He has a medical history of coughs and chest infections.'

'Serious?'

'Serious enough for his GP to have prescribed several courses of antibiotics.' He frowned. 'According to his case notes, from the age of three the little chap has had recurring incidences of headaches and high temperatures.'

'Poor little thing.'

Callum nodded. He put his cup down to hunt for the case notes again and leaned against the work surface. 'According to this…' he tapped the card with his finger '…Daniel had an inflammation of the mastoid bone.'

'That's nasty. Did they operate?'

'Yes—as an emergency. A year later the problem recurred and he needed more surgery. He made a slow recovery.'

Holly frowned. 'I take it you've seen him recently?'

'His mother brought him to the surgery for the first time about two months ago. I examined him. He had a chest infection and I prescribed more antibiotics.'

Holly looked at him. 'You're obviously not happy about it.'

'Would you be?'

'No,' she admitted, frowning, 'but I don't see that you had any other choice.'

'Neither did I at the time.' His brows drew together. 'It was only when his mother turned up with Daniel again at the surgery a couple of weeks ago that I began to realise there may be more to it. That I might be missing something important.'

Holly stared at him. 'Like what?'

'Like a wrong diagnosis. A series of wrong diagnoses.'

She gave a slight laugh. 'You're not serious?'

'It's the only answer.' He frowned. 'Daniel last had surgery twelve months ago. Since the family moved into the area six months ago, I've seen Daniel three times. Each time he had an ear infection, severe enough to warrant giving more antibiotics. And he's seriously underweight.'

Callum straightened up, reaching for his coffee. 'I decided it was time to do some tests.'

'And?'

'The results came through this morning.' He sounded quietly angry. 'Daniel has CF.'

'Cystic fibrosis?'

His mouth tightened. 'Children with CF have high levels of salt in their sweat so it's easy to diagnose. It just took so bloody long to think of it—to make the connection between his illnesses.'

She gave a slight laugh. 'Hey, come on. That's hardly your fault!'

'I'm not sure that makes me feel any better. When I think of what that five-year-old has been going through. Cystic fibrosis means his lungs get clogged up with mucus, which is why he's so prone to infection and damage, and the mucus blocks the production of food-digesting enzymes.'

'Which explains why he's so underweight,' Holly said softly.

Callum grimaced. 'Someone should have spotted what was going on.'

'Someone did. *You* did. At least now the problem has been identified Daniel can start having appropriate treatment.'

'It doesn't quite end there though, does it? I still have to talk to Daniel's parents, explain to them that not only does their son have cystic fibrosis but that the condition is inherited. Which means that their other child will also have to be tested.'

Holly could see now why he had appeared so testy when she had walked into Reception. Clearly she wasn't the only one who found there were some aspects of this job that were unpleasant.

'You once told me that we can't perform miracles,' she reminded him gently. She put her coffee-cup down and reached for her briefcase. 'I really do have to make a start.'

Callum looked at his watch and followed her to the door. 'At this rate I'll still be here at lunchtime.' He pulled open the door and walked out of Reception. In a moment or two a buzzer sounded and the receptionist called for the first patient to go along to his room.

Holly gave a little sigh and turned towards the desk to smile at Fiona. 'I suppose it will help if I have a list of the visits I'm supposed to make.'

Fiona hunted through an assortment of papers. 'I know it's here somewhere. Ah, here we are.' She handed over the paper.

Holly scanned the list and gave a groan. 'All for me?'

'Every last one.'

Holly pulled a wry face. 'Dr McLoud isn't the only one who'll be busy till lunchtime. I should have brought a packed lunch.'

'At least he's in a better mood now,' Fiona said in a low mutter. 'He's been like a bear with a sore head since he arrived this morning. He used to frighten me to death,' she confided, 'but that was before I got to know him and the way he works. He certainly doesn't suffer fools gladly.'

Holly could believe it. She gave a noncommittal smile.

'I can't help thinking it's a good thing he isn't married, though. His wife would need the patience of a saint.' Fiona mused on that thought for a while. 'Mind you, perhaps marriage would mellow him a little, don't you think?'

'I shouldn't think there's much likelihood of that happening in the near future.' Holly swiftly disabused her of the idea as she checked her day's schedule in her diary.

Fiona pulled a wry face. 'You're probably right. I heard he was engaged once. But things didn't work out. There hasn't been anyone since then, as far as I know.' She grinned. 'A case of once bitten twice shy, I shouldn't wonder.'

Holly managed a faint smile, but Fiona's words echoed

her own thoughts almost exactly, at least as far as any permanent relationship was concerned. She glanced at her watch. 'Could you ring the hospital for me some time this morning and check on how Mrs McGiver is? I had to get her admitted last night and I'm worried about her.'

'I'll see to it.'

'We may need to organise some help for Mr McGiver as well. I'll chat to someone about it when I get back.'

It was a busy morning and some three hours later before Holly was finally able to head back to the surgery. She felt tired and cold.

The waiting room was empty and she made her way through to Reception where she dropped her briefcase onto the desk, before blowing on her hands.

'Lor, it's freezing out there.'

Agnes Ferguson glanced anxiously out of the window at the leaden sky. 'From the look of things, I'd say we'll have more snow by morning.' She glanced at Holly. 'You wanted news of Mrs McGiver.'

'Oh, yes, that's right.'

'I have it here somewhere.' Agnes riffled through the cluttered surface of the desk. 'Ah, yes, here we are.' She handed over the piece of paper. 'They say she had a comfortable night.' Agnes shook her head disapprovingly. 'I dare say the poor woman might disagree. Oh, and these are for signing, Doctor. I'll get them in the post this evening.'

'Fine.' Reaching for a pen, Holly scrawled her signature. 'I've got a couple of letters of referral as well, I'm afraid. No rush. Tomorrow will do. One is to Mr Jameson.'

She frowned. 'I want to get young Stevie Wallace in to see him as soon as possible. His hearing is getting pretty bad. He really needs to have grommets in his ears before he starts school, otherwise he'll soon start to fall behind with his lessons.'

'Aye, well, I know his mother will be pleased about that.'

'And there's… Oh, here we are. This one is to Mr Buchanan.'

'That'll be the orthopaedic chappie.'

'That's the one.' Holly opened her briefcase and searched through the case notes. 'I want to see if there's any chance of bringing Sam Hopkins's operation forward. The poor man is just about at the end of his tether with those knees of his and I can't say I blame him.'

She straightened up. 'I don't suppose you know if Kirsty is still around?'

'Still in the treatment room, I think.' Agnes scanned the appointments book. 'Yes, her last patient left about ten minutes ago.'

'Great.' Holly smiled. 'I'll pop in to see her before she dashes off for lunch.' The mere thought was enough to set her own stomach rumbling, but she tried to ignore it as she made her way along the corridor.

Tapping at one of the doors, she opened it and popped her head round. 'Hi! Can I have a word or is this a bad time?'

Kirsty Sinclair, the dark-haired practice nurse looked up and smiled. 'No, it's fine. I was just clearing up. Here, let me move those magazines then you can sit down.'

'No, I'm fine, really. I was hoping to get away before it gets dark. At this rate I doubt I'll make it. I really wanted to ask how we're doing for supplies of MMR vaccine. I know we've had a bit of a run on them lately since that last outbreak of measles. We had a couple of cases of mumps at the local school a couple of weeks ago, too.'

'It's OK.' Kirsty smiled. 'I checked supplies yesterday. I think we've enough.'

'Oh, well, that's fine. At least I can sleep easy in my

bed. I wouldn't want it on my conscience if the entire school went down with the dreaded lurgy.'

'No chance.' Kirsty grinned. 'Most of the mums around here are pretty responsible. They bring the babies in to have the injection. A few of them don't like to, of course, but I always point out that a few seconds of discomfort are better than running the risk of their babies actually getting the German measles, especially the girls.'

She looked up from the boxes of supplies she was checking. 'I heard about poor Mrs McGiver, by the way. She was admitted to hospital, is that right?'

'Yes, I'm afraid so. She had a subarachnoid haemorrhage.'

'Oh, the poor wee thing. Will they operate?'

'I'm not sure. Obviously the neurosurgeon will make his decision based on the severity of her condition. I understand that they did a lumbar puncture to confirm the presence of blood. But I doubt they would contemplate operating for several weeks, until the acute episode has settled down.'

Kirsty nodded. 'It's going to be an awful time for poor Mr McGiver. They're such a nice couple.'

Holly frowned. 'That the other reason I wanted to see you. I know he's worried about his wife. I imagine he'll want to spend as much time as possible at the hospital with her, but he's seventy and I get the impression he tends to rely on his wife when it comes to things like cooking and cleaning.'

'You think he needs some sort of support?'

Holly nodded. 'It might be a good idea.'

'I'll get on to it if you like.'

'Would you? You're an angel. Oh, lor! Look at the time. I'd better get a move on. The mountain of paperwork on my desk seems to grow higher by the day.'

Holly went out of the office and walked along the corridor. As she passed Callum's room the door was open. He was standing with his back to her, stacking books onto a shelf.

On impulse she paused and tapped at the door. 'Could I have a quick word with you before you leave?' she asked.

'Is it important? I was just about to make a start on my visits.' He didn't look any too pleased at the prospect of being delayed but, having taken the initiative, it was too late for her to have second thoughts now.

'It's about David Galbraith,' she told him. 'I mentioned him to you. The patient with suspected prostate cancer?'

'Yes, I remember. So what point are you trying to make?'

Holly took a quick sharp breath at his impatient tone. She had obviously chosen the wrong moment to ask him anything. 'I got the hospital report yesterday. It confirmed my diagnosis.'

Callum frowned. 'I'm sorry. You'll start him on a course of treatment?'

'Obviously.' Holly sighed. 'I just wish we were fighting against better odds, that's all.' She looked at him. 'I've been thinking. The display of leaflets in the waiting room was a good idea and I'm really grateful to you for thinking of it.'

'But?'

She frowned. 'I just keep getting the feeling that it isn't enough. Maybe we could do more to get over the message about prostate cancer and the fact that it is treatable, provided it's caught in the early stages.'

'What did you have in mind?'

'Well, for a start, why can't we have a few posters made to display in Reception and the waiting room? And perhaps we could make available a confidential phone line so that if someone does have any worries they can at least talk to someone about it.'

Callum leaned across the desk to switch off his computer. 'You know that no matter how much information we give out, we can't force patients to take advice?'

Her chin rose determinedly. 'Yes, of course, I realise that. But if we can reach even one person out there who may have fears about prostate cancer, and persuade them to come and at least talk to us, it will have been worth it.'

She hesitated and Callum sent her an oblique glance. 'Why do I get the feeling there's more?'

Holly frowned. 'I was thinking of setting up a meeting one evening, inviting patients, not necessarily just the male patients—their wives, too, if they want to come—to hear someone speak to them about prostate problems.'

'Go on.'

'Maybe we could get a consultant from the local hospital to come along. It could be an informal affair, and they would have a chance to ask questions. I'd be willing to give up some free time to be there. What do you think?'

'Sounds like a good idea to me.' Holly barely had time to be astonished by his swift agreement before he went on, 'It might be worth considering setting it up on a regular basis. Once a month, say. Go ahead and arrange it. We'll see what sort of response there is and take it from there.'

Callum started towards the door, and she followed him slowly. He stopped suddenly and threw her a sharp glance. 'Why so surprised?' he said. 'What did you expect me to say?'

Holly gave him a faint smile. 'I wasn't sure. You've seemed quite remote this last few days.'

'Remote?' His mouth curved in a wry response. 'I was trying to keep things on a strictly professional basis between us because I thought that was what you wanted. Was I wrong, Holly?'

She stared at him and wished she hadn't as her eyes

encountered his mouth, firm and attractive and far too much of a threat to her peace of mind.

He went on thoughtfully, 'I don't think you know what you *do* want, Holly. I know you've had a difficult time over the past couple of years, but life has to move on.'

She moistened her dry lips with her tongue. 'I'm sure you're right. It just isn't that easy—'

'I'm not saying it is,' he cut in. 'I'm not saying you should forget, or that you shouldn't feel some sense of loyalty to the past. But what about you, Holly? Don't you owe it to yourself to make a new life? To use the talents you were given? Isn't that what Tony would have wanted?'

'You don't understand.'

'I'm trying to.' His gaze narrowed. 'What is it that you're so afraid of, Holly? You have no reason to feel guilty for wanting to be happy, for getting on with your own life.'

Holly stared at him in wide-eyed, open-mouthed astonishment. He had recognised her fears when she had scarcely even voiced them to herself, let alone to anyone else.

Callum's fingers moved to brush gently against her cheek. 'Close your mouth,' he said, his voice rough around the edges. 'Unless you want me to kiss it again.'

She closed her mouth promptly, gulping in a swift, sharp breath. He said drily, 'You're as tense as a wound spring. You need to unwind, discover what it is to relax again...and I know of just the thing.'

He released her. 'Alex and Irene are having a little pre-Christmas party at their son's house. He's obviously feeling better and it will do him good to see everyone again. All the staff from the practice are invited, and that includes you.'

'No, I can't,' Holly began. She could feel the familiar sense of panic rising. 'My clothes…'

'Will be just fine.' Callum looked stern. 'I'm warning you now, Holly,' he said quietly. 'I'll not see Alex and Irene offended by a refusal. He's looking forward to meeting you and thanking you properly for standing in for him. So you'll go to this party if I have to carry you there myself.'

He started towards the door once more. 'And now that we've settled that little matter satisfactorily,' he murmured, 'I'd better get on with my visits. At this rate I'll not be back before dark and I've still to take an evening surgery.'

'Satisfactorily?' she echoed. 'But I haven't said—' She broke off as he returned to plant a kiss firmly on her soft mouth, and she felt the tingle of it reverberate right through her, down to her toes.

'Keep arguing and I shall have to keep kissing, Holly.' A smile tilted his mouth, and she felt the colour flare into her cheeks. 'I'll see you again to talk about the arrangements.'

He moved away from her and, dazedly, she stared after him, a strangely unnerving sensation coursing through her limbs and leaving her feeling oddly helpless.

CHAPTER SEVEN

HOLLY didn't want to discuss arrangements for the Douglases' party. For the best part of a week she had tried to come up with an excuse for not going, and finally had to acknowledge that there was no way she was going to get out of it. But she definitely wasn't looking forward to it.

The idea of meeting people, of having to be sociable, filled her with a sense of dread, and it didn't make it any easier that everyone else was looking forward to the party. Alex Douglas and his wife were obviously a popular couple, and the talk in the practice seemed to revolve around little else but the forthcoming event until Holly felt like blocking her ears with cotton wool.

Another thought crept in too as she sat, staring out of the window at the dancing flakes of snow. If Alex was, indeed, feeling so much better, he must be planning to return to work at the practice shortly.

It came as something of a shock to realise what it meant and her heart gave a sudden extra thud. Her job here would be at an end. She would be free to leave. Callum was right, she knew that— she had to get on with her life. But picking up the threads, it wouldn't be that easy.

Yes, she had managed to cope, to fit in, here in this small, tightly knit community. But what about when she had to start again somewhere else?

It was strange that even in the space of a few weeks everything that had gone before seemed suddenly like some distant, almost forgotten part of her life, as if they belonged to an altogether different world—which they did.

A world, she suddenly realised, which didn't include Callum McLoud.

She blinked a sudden and totally illogical misting of tears from her eyes and rose to her feet to replace a book on the shelf. Her movements seemed oddly disjointed. She had quite enough to occupy her thoughts, without letting her imagination run away with her where Callum was concerned.

Reaching for her bag, she went through to Reception, where she handed over the morning's batch of case notes, before heading for the staffroom.

It had been a busy and unusually trying morning. What she needed right now, she decided, was coffee, hot, strong and very sweet, and a chance to unwind, if only temporarily.

In the staffroom she found Jamie, helping himself to coffee, and Kirsty, already seated, glancing through a magazine.

'We were just wondering whether to send out a search party,' they told her.

Holly smiled. 'Don't worry. I've been looking forward to this for the past hour. Mmm, I'm ready for this.'

'I know the feeling.' Jamie handed her a cup. 'It's been one of those days. I even managed to lose a patient.'

'Oh, no! You don't mean…?'

'Lord, no. Nothing quite so drastic, thank goodness. I mean lost as in mislaid.' He helped himself to another biscuit. 'I sent old Ian Forsyth off to provide me with a urine specimen. Fifteen minutes later, when he still hadn't returned, I had to go looking for him. The poor old chap was having a bit of a problem.'

'What did you do?' Kirsty glanced at him over her magazine.

'Turned on the taps and gave him a nice cup of tea.'

'Ah, well.' Holly grinned. 'As long as it produced the right result.'

Jamie grabbed another biscuit, before handing the plate to Holly. 'As long as the rest of the patients don't start asking for refreshments, too, otherwise we're in trouble. Anyway, it's all right for some. The rest of us have to do some work.' And he was gone, grinning as a magazine flew through the air—missing him by inches.

Holly sank into a chair, easing off her shoes.

'Bad morning?'

'Oh, actually it wasn't too bad.' Holly leaned back, relishing the hot coffee. 'If you discount the requests for antibiotics when you know an aspirin, or even a dram of whisky, would do the trick.' Briefly she closed her eyes.

'They say it gets easier. Mind you, they don't say when.'

'I'm relieved to hear it.' Holly relaxed, smiling, and found herself wondering whether she would be here long enough to found out whether it got easier. The thought left her feeling oddly depressed.

'I heard about your idea for a series of group meetings, by the way.' Kirsty set her magazine aside. 'Callum sounded me out about it. I think it's a good idea. We have a Well Woman clinic so why not the equivalent, offering advice to men on prostate problems, or any other problem?' She nodded. 'I'm all for it.'

'Oh, I'm glad.'

Kirsty poured more coffee. 'In fact, I don't know why someone didn't think of it before.'

'To tell you the truth, I wasn't exactly sure the idea would be welcomed.'

'For heaven's sake, why? Callum was impressed.' Kirsty shot a glance in Holly's direction. 'He's really not quite the ogre he may sometimes seem, you know? I mean, really, deep down he's soft as butter.'

Holly swallowed a mouthful of hot coffee, feeling it

burn her throat as the cup rattled into the saucer. 'Yes, well, I think I'll reserve judgement, if you don't mind.'

Kirsty grinned and was handing her empty cup to Holly when the door opened and Callum walked in, a harassed expression marring his attractive features. 'Talk of the devil. My cue to exit, I think,' muttered Kirsty, making her excuses and slipping away.

'I seem to spend most of my time battling my way through paperwork these days.' There was a taut edge to Callum's voice. 'I sometimes think I should have been an accountant instead of a doctor! If you're doing the honours, I'll have mine black with three sugars.'

A small pulse began to hammer in Holly's throat as she rose to her feet to pour more coffee. 'I know what you mean,' she murmured, willing her hands to remain steady as she handed him the cup.

As he took it their fingers met, evoking so vivid a memory of the moments she had spent in his arms that she jerked away, spilling coffee into the saucer.

He was wearing dark trousers and a white shirt. She found herself gazing with fascination at the tanned column of his throat, before her gaze rose to meet the full impact of his startlingly blue eyes.

'Sleep well?' he asked.

'Fine, thanks.' She took several deep breaths, hoping he would put the sudden bright colour in her cheeks down to the hot coffee she had just swallowed.

She turned away, put her cup down and briefly closed her eyes. Why was it that she only had to be near this man for her entire nervous system to go completely haywire?

She took a deep breath. 'By the way, I wanted—'

'Holly, I—' She turned, gasping as she collided heavily with his solid, masculine frame, and found herself staring into his frowning gaze.

'Oh.' She could smell the faint aroma of his aftershave,

feel his heart beating against hers, but it was the illogical sense of longing that surged through her which caused her lips to part slightly.

She heard his sharp intake of breath, saw his eyes widen too, before she swiftly extricated herself from his arms, all too annoyingly aware that she was blushing even more.

'I…I'm sorry. I didn't see you standing there.'

'Think nothing of it. As a matter of fact, I was rather hoping I'd bump into you.' His eyes glinted. 'About the party.'

'Yes, look…' She swallowed hard. 'I've been meaning to talk to you. I really can't—'

'It's all right. That's what I wanted to tell you. I've already spoken to Alex and Irene and accepted on your behalf.' He glanced, frowning, at his watch. 'They're both looking forward to meeting you.'

'But you can't. You had no right.' She stared at him and was furiously summoning an argument when Jamie erupted back into the room. It occurred to her to wonder whether he ever moved at a normal pace.

'Callum,' he said cheerily, 'I thought you'd like to know that you were right. Bridie Stevenson's blood tests did show up positive for sugar. I've left a copy of the report on your desk.

Grinning, he looked at Holly. 'By the way, I heard about your idea for setting up a series of discussion groups on prostate problems.'

She gave a slight laugh. 'Groups, meetings, drop-in sessions. I haven't even got around to work out the best way to deal with it yet.'

'Well, I'm all in favour. I just wanted you to know. If you need any help, just give me a call. Oh, and if you'd like an escort to the Douglases' party on Saturday night, I'm ready and willing and promise to have the coach wait-

ing. Furthermore, you have my assurance that I'll not turn
into a rat come the stroke of midnight.'

Holly chuckled. She couldn't help it. Jamie Nichols was
an outrageous flirt but as he made no bones about it she
knew it was quite harmless.

Suddenly, without turning her head, she could feel the
weight of Callum's eyes watching her, a frown suddenly
darkening his gaze.

'Well, I—' she began.

'Aren't you supposed to be on call that evening, Dr
Nichols?'

The set of Callum's mouth suggested that he was angry
and Holly wondered why. Then suddenly it hit her that
perhaps he disapproved of mixing business with pleasure.

She managed to keep her voice even as she smiled at
Jamie. 'It's nice of you to offer, but it really doesn't matter.'

'It's no problem.' He grinned, unabashed, and reached
into his pocket, holding aloft his mobile phone. 'The won-
ders of modern science are many and great. Isn't that right,
Callum?'

Holly saw the dark brows come down and from
Callum's thunderous expression could tell that he was fu-
rious. On the other hand, a spark of rebellion asserted itself. Just because he was her boss, that didn't give him the
right to organise her social life as well. And since it
seemed she had no choice but to go to this party anyway,
thanks to him...

She flashed him a look, before bestowing her brightest
smile on Jamie. 'In that case I shall look forward to it.'

The firm set of Callum's mouth suggested that she was
treading on dangerous ground. But then she had become
accustomed to that of late.

It was a pity that her resolve had weakened by the time
her day off came around. As the day of the party drew

nearer she began to get more and more nervous, not least over what she was going to wear.

Later that evening she surveyed the meagre contents of her wardrobe. The result was as depressing as she had expected. There was nothing else for it—she was going to have to splash out on something new.

As luck would have it, the following day was her day off and the sun was making a determined effort to shine as, dressed in brown trousers, a bright red sweater and a warm jacket, she took herself into town.

It was still early when, having locked the car, she headed for the main shopping area. Buying one dress, that shouldn't take too long, she told herself. It should leave ample time for all the chores she had been planning to do but never quite seemed to get round to.

What she hadn't counted on were the brightly-lit, festively decked boutiques, and it dawned on her, with a sudden sense of shock, that Christmas was only a few weeks away.

Somehow the past two Christmases had passed almost unnoticed, certainly unacknowledged, because to have done so would have been to resurrect too many bad memories. Which was perhaps why she now found herself gazing in fascination at the goods displayed so invitingly in the shop windows.

She hadn't actually meant to go in, just to look. Then she had spotted the dress and before she knew what was happening somehow she was trying it on.

'It's a perfect fit,' the saleslady enthused, standing behind Holly to stare in the mirror. 'It might have made specially for you. And that shade of green is just perfect. It's an almost exact match for your eyes.' Her voice contained a faint note of envy which was completely lost on Holly.

This wasn't at all what she had intended to buy, but the

sales assistant was right about the fit at least. In recent weeks she had begun to regain some of the lost weight.

Turning so that she could view the back, Holly studied the line of the figure-hugging dress and had to admit that it did look good.

In the end, what should have been a quick trip took up several hours and left her footsore, not to mention considerably short in the pocket.

Zipping herself into the dress on Saturday evening, she looked at herself carefully in the mirror and experienced a new tremor of anxiety. Had she made a mistake in buying it?

Mac lay with his chin on his paws, eyebrows twitching, as she tugged, frowning, at the hem of the dress.

'All right, so what do you think? Too short? Not short enough?' She ruffled the Westie's fur. 'Fat lot of help you are.'

A thin diamanté halter gave an illusion of safety. Even so, she wasn't sure there ought to be quite so much bareness about the shoulders.

She was applying touches of her favourite perfume to her pulse points when, right on cue, the doorbell rang. That would be Jamie.

Slipping her feet into slender-heeled sandals, Holly reached for her evening purse and, with Mac scampering at her heels, went to open the door.

'Come in. I just have to get my jacket and check that I left Mac some water. Help yourself to a drink. I won't be—' She broke off, feeling a rush of heat and cold all at the same time as Callum studied her with penetrating intensity.

She felt the glittering sweep of his blue eyes flame over the creamy translucence of her bare shoulders to the curve of her breasts.

'You!' She swallowed convulsively on the sudden tightness in her throat. 'I was expecting Jamie.'

'Sorry to disappoint you,' he said evenly. 'Something
came up. A bit of an emergency at the last minute.' Holly
wondered if she had imagined the note of satisfaction in
his voice. 'He asked me to make his apologies.'

CHAPTER EIGHT

HOLLY passed her tongue over her dry lips, intensely aware of Callum and the effect his nearness was having on her.

If she had thought him attractive before he was devastatingly so now in the more formal dark suit.

She swallowed hard. I…er, you'd better come in.' He followed as she headed for the small sitting room. She hesitated in the open doorway. 'I'm almost ready. Can I offer you a drink before we go? I'm afraid I don't keep much alcohol but there's some sherry—'

She broke off, aware of his penetrating gaze raking her slowly from head to toe, lingering with disturbing intensity on the narrowness of her waist and hips—all, she realised now, accentuated by the softness of the clinging fabric.

Panic hit her. He didn't like the dress! She stared down at it. 'Is…is something wrong…? With the dress, I mean? Is it too formal?' She looked at him. 'I could go and change. It won't take a minute.'

'You look beautiful, Holly,' Callum put in softly. 'I think we'd better forget the drink.'

'Oh, yes, of course.' She glanced anxiously at her watch. 'I hadn't realised we were late.'

She reached for her jacket. Callum moved to help her, his fingers warm on the soft curve of her shoulders. She might have been naked to his touch and the sensation startled her in its intensity, making her nerves jump in riotous disorder.

'We're not *yet*,' he said tautly.

He released her slowly. Holly swallowed hard, her

113

breathing uneven as he ushered her towards the car, opening the passenger door and helping her in before going
round to the driver's seat.

It wasn't a small car, but he was still far too close and
still the most sexually exciting man she had ever met.

An involuntary shiver ran through her and, as if instantly
aware of it, he took his eyes from the road to glance at
her.

'Nervous?'

She *was*, but not for the reason he was thinking. 'A
little.'

'There's no need to be, you know. Alex and Irene are
fine people. They have some very nice friends.'

'I'm sure they have.' She avoided his gaze, glad that he
had mistaken the real reason behind that shiver. His nearness was affecting her in a way she hadn't dreamed possible, and it was seriously undermining her resolve never
to allow herself to feel this vulnerable ever again.

It was a relief when they drew up outside the house and
she was able to climb out of the car.

'I'm so glad you could come.' Irene Douglas greeted
their arrival with obvious pleasure. A slim, petite woman
of about sixty, her attractive features were emphasised by
a modern-style haircut and the soft angora, cowl-necked
dress she was wearing.

She raised her voice above the sound of music. 'I know
it's ridiculous but I feel so nervous,' she confided with a
smile as she led them into the house. 'I don't know why
I let myself in for this sort of thing.'

'It's not every day you celebrate forty years of marriage.' Callum smiled. He handed her a large bouquet of
flowers and bent his head to kiss her cheek. 'Happy an-
niversary, Irene. I wish you many more.'

'Oh, aren't they gorgeous?' Irene inhaled their fra-
grance, then, smiling, took Holly's hand. 'My dear, come

through and have a drink. You must come and meet every-one, including Alex. He's in there somewhere,' she said wryly.

'How is he now?' Callum said.

'Much, much better, and I'm so grateful to you, my dear.' She looked at Holly. 'Alex's heart attack was a great shock to us all. He's always been such an active man. He's not been a good patient, I'm afraid. But, then, they say doctors never are.'

She smiled slightly. 'I was so afraid he wouldn't behave sensibly and take things more easily but, I have to say, he seems to have taken to convalescence far better than I'd hoped. He's actually been happier and feels more reas-sured, knowing that the practice is ticking along so nicely without him. At least he doesn't feel so guilty about leav-ing you all to cope.'

'There's no need for him to feel guilty.' Callum smiled. 'We miss him, but we want him to take his time and get really well.'

'He'll enjoy talking to you and catching up on all the latest gossip.' Irene smiled as she ushered them ahead of her. 'I won't even attempt to introduce you formally to everyone. I'm not even certain I know all their names my-self,' she confided. 'I certainly don't recall inviting quite so many people.'

Callum said, 'You're a popular lady, and Alex isn't without a fair number of good friends, too.'

The doorbell rang. Irene flung a smiling look of apology in their direction. 'My dears, do go in while I see who that is.'

There were certainly more people than she had ex-pected, Holly thought as they edged their way into the crowded lounge.

The room was filled with chattering groups and someone

was circulating between them with trays of chilled white wine and fruit juice.

Holly stood in the doorway, conscious of a sudden tension in her limbs, a feeling of panic which made her want to draw away. Just when she had thought she was beginning to get her feelings about Tony into some kind of perspective, the memories came back to haunt her. Suddenly, the thought of walking into that room, of meeting those people, was too much.

Rationally she knew it was crazy to feel this way, but irrationally, for those few fleeting seconds, the panic still rose, threatening to choke her.

Without even being aware of it, she had half turned, her eyes widening, only to feel the gentle but firm pressure of Callum's hand beneath her elbow.

'Are you all right?' Blue eyes looked down into hers.

She swallowed hard on the tightness in her throat, the momentary fear vanishing, to be replaced by a sudden and far more tangible awareness of the man standing beside her.

A tremor of desire ran through her as Callum's dark eyes travelled over her. Her body responded as he touched her, sending a wave of heat rushing through her. His sexual magnetism took her breath away. Almost everything about him took her breath away!

It was ridiculous to feel safe with someone who, in every other sense, seemed to represent a threat, even though she couldn't have said precisely what that threat was. But the feel of his hand against her back was like a protective shield, drawing her to him, shutting everyone else out.

'I should have warned you about the crush.' His brow furrowed. 'I'd better lead the way.'

Holly followed, taking several deep breaths and releasing them shakily. Almost immediately Callum was waylaid, and involuntarily she found herself searching for his dark head in the crowd.

'Holly!' A glass of wine was thrust into her hand. 'We've been keeping an eye open for you.' It was Fiona, her face flushed, her eyes unusually bright. 'We were hoping you'd make it. This is Craig, by the way.'

Holly found herself shaking hands with a tall, fair-haired young man.

'Hello. It's nice to meet you.' She smiled.

'Same here. I've heard a lot about you.'

Holly glanced at Fiona, who grinned. 'Don't worry. it was all good. Actually…' she flushed '…Craig and I are engaged.'

'Oh, that's great news.'

Fiona lowered her voice to a confiding whisper. 'Only we haven't told anyone else yet. We've only just decided to make it official, so we're waiting until we've had a chance to break the news to the families before telling everyone else.'

'Well, I'm flattered, and delighted, to be the first to hear the news.' Holly raised her glass to the smiling couple.

'Have you had any food yet?'

'Not yet.' She had to raise her voice above the noise, gazing in admiration at the buffet. 'It looks wonderful. Almost too good to eat.'

'Our Irene is quite a cook on the quiet.'

'Any party given by the Douglases and you can guarantee people will be falling over themselves to get an invitation. Just lead me to the coronation chicken.' Fiona laughed as they joined the crush around the table, Holly helping herself to food she didn't really want.

As the evening progressed, the lights were dimmed and soft music was drifting from a CD unit in the corner of the room. Several couples were dancing slowly, swaying together in time to the music.

Unconsciously, Holly found herself searching for Callum. She saw him, deeply engrossed in conversation with Alex Douglas and a small group of guests.

She found herself watching, fascinated, as he smiled down at the woman beside him. Diminutive, blonde-haired, she had the kind of flawless, honeyed skin that any woman would envy.

'Well, well,' Fiona said softly. 'Fancy that. I'd no idea Sarah was going to be here.'

'Sarah?' With an effort, Holly forced her attention to the girl beside her.

'But, of course, you wouldn't know. That's Sarah Munro. The girl Callum was engaged to. I haven't seen her in Glenloch since she married and moved away.'

'From the look of things, I'd say they're still pretty close,' Holly remarked, trying to keep her tone light and even and wondering why her heart was suddenly hammering inside her chest.

The girl turned her head to look up at Callum and he shook his head. His hand rested briefly, reassuringly, on her shoulder. Watching, Holly felt the fierce stab of something she refused to acknowledge as jealousy moving down her spine.

'You could be right,' Fiona agreed. 'I was never sure—none of us were—what caused them to break up. Everyone thought she and Callum would marry. They'd known each other since they were children.' She frowned. 'Next thing we knew, the engagement was off and she had married his best friend.'

'You mean…her husband is here?'

'Oh, no.' Fiona turned her head to look at her. 'Didn't I say? The poor man died. Apparently it was quite sudden. They thought he had flu but…well, it turned out to be something more serious.' She glanced around and a grin broke out. 'Uh-oh. Here comes trouble.'

Holly did her best to drag her attention away from the absorbed couple and tried to concentrate on what Fiona was saying.

The sight of Callum's hand, proprietorially against Sarah Munro's back as he led her gently through the crowd, made the breath snag in Holly's throat. Why should it bother her that they should want to be alone and unobserved?

She forced herself to look away and concentrate on Jamie, looking hot and slightly harassed, standing beside her.

'I wondered where you were hiding.' Grinning, he whisked the glass out of Holly's hand and swept her, laughing, into his arms. 'I've come to offer my apologies for not bringing you to the party, and to claim my dance.' He executed an intricate jumble of steps, whirling her round.

'I'm not sure I'm up to this,' she protested.

'Neither am I.' He grinned again. 'So, we've got the twiddly bits out of the way, now we can relax.'

And there was something nice and safe about an old-fashioned slow dance, she decided, settling into the comfortable circle of Jamie's arms as they made steady progress around the floor. Nothing too demanding, either physically or emotionally.

'By the way, you won't forget my offer of help, will you? I meant it, you know.'

'No, I won't, and I'm grateful. I think I'm going to need all the support I can get.'

'What's the response been so far?'

'Surprisingly good,' she told him, adding hurriedly, 'Though that's not to say everyone who's made enquiries will turn up on the evening.'

'Callum is fully behind you on the idea, you know, and he's a pretty shrewd judge of these things. He wouldn't back you unless he was sure it would be a success and that it would benefit the patients.'

She was pleased to hear it, even if she wasn't entirely convinced. And the real work, the hard work, was yet to come—she knew that. It was one thing to come up with an idea, but she still had to prove that it could work. However, for tonight at least she wasn't going to think about that.

Smiling wryly, she looked up at Jamie. 'I'm still not even sure what format to use. I mean, obviously we need to keep it fairly informal. We don't want to frighten people off before we've even had a chance to talk to them.'

'Tell you what.' Jamie neatly executed a turn. 'Why don't we get together one evening and discuss it? How about over dinner?'

'Oh, well…'

'Fine. I'll take that as a yes.' He snuggled closer, his cheek against her own.

For the next ten minutes Holly gave herself up to the rhythm of the music and found, to her surprise, that she was actually enjoying herself. Jamie was a good dancer and, despite the lack of space, she was able to fit her steps to his so that they were soon moving together with an easy familiarity.

He swung her around as the fast disco beat faded to a conclusion, his hand resting lightly on her hip, and she looked up at him and smiled widely.

'I haven't danced like that in a long time,' she said breathlessly. She felt exhilarated, freed from all the tensions of the last weeks…years even.

'You should smile more often. It suits you.' Jamie studied her, his glance flickering appreciatively over the flush in her cheeks and the pink, full curve of her mouth. 'Perhaps we could do this again some time? When we're both off duty—'

'I think maybe you've monopolised Holly for long enough, don't you?'

She was suddenly aware of Callum's hand coming to rest against her bare back, the warmth of his fingers stirring her senses in a way she knew to be totally illogical.

He stared down at her, and her already overworked pulse rate accelerated dangerously. 'I think we should dance, don't you?' His mouth made a firm, uncompromising line.

Reluctantly, Jamie relinquished her hand to Callum. She swayed, caution telling her to keep her distance, while instinct and the pressure of his hand over her fingers broke down her fragile defences.

Holly's breathing felt constricted as they moved into the crowd. Why did this man have such an effect on her? It was like nothing she had ever experienced before. And why did someone have to choose that precise moment to put on a slow piece of music so that, rather than dancing apart, he was drawing her closer, moulding her against his rugged frame.

'You're annoyed,' she said, sensing the tension in him as he moved. 'Why? Is it something I've done—or said?'

His jaw clenched fractionally. 'I thought the idea of coming to a party was to mingle, to get to know people.'

She stiffened defensively, emboldened by the glass of wine. 'I thought I was here to have fun. Besides, I'm surprised you had time to notice what I was doing. You seemed to be enjoying yourself.' She couldn't resist the jibe. 'Has your friend gone?'

'Friend?'

'Sarah? Is that her name? Fiona mentioned that you two had been engaged.'

One dark brow rose quizzically. 'Sarah used to live close by. When the Douglases knew she was visiting Glenloch, naturally enough they invited her along to their party.

It seemed the perfect opportunity for her to meet old friends.'

'Yes, of course. I see.' She went on cautiously. 'It must have been nice to meet up again. You're obviously still friends. Things can't have been easy after you split up, or…?'

'Sarah and I have been friends for a long time. We still are.' He shifted restlessly, his hand firming on her spine. 'Are we going to argue, or shall we relax and enjoy the music?'

She realised she must have touched on a sore point, but if he chose not to talk about his ex-fiancée, she was happy to go along with that. It wasn't so easy to relax, not when she could feel the heat of him, the thin fabric of her dress no barrier at all, when she was vibrantly conscious of every move he made.

His jacket brushed softly against her cheek. It smelled of expensive cologne and her skin tingled as he turned his head, his sensuous mouth close to her cheek.

'Relax,' he said softly. 'At least try to look as if you're enjoying yourself.'

Confusion brought the faint colour to her cheeks and she swallowed hard, her mouth strangely dry as she was held within the intimate circle of his arms.

She was trying, but his proximity was making that impossible. Holly drew a long, shaky breath. The music would have to be soft and romantic, wouldn't it? Just when he had chosen to claim her for a dance. She knew it had to be coincidence, of course. He wouldn't have arranged it that way.

No, that was pure fanciful thinking on her part. He was at a loose end now that Sarah had gone, that was all. And the thought disturbed her far more than she cared to admit.

She stirred uneasily in his arms. 'It's getting late,' she said. 'I should be going. I'm on duty in the morning.'

'I'll take you home. it won't take a moment to say our goodbyes to Alex and Irene.'

Her breathing was ragged as he drew her away from the slowly moving dancers. 'There's no need, really. Jamie will be leaving soon. I can get a lift.'

'Why disturb him when he's enjoying himself?' He glanced at his watch. 'We've done our duty. I think we can safely bow out, don't you?'

But she wasn't sure she wanted to leave with him. There was suddenly a lot to be said for safety in numbers.

Callum swept her to a halt at the spot where Alex and Irene were standing, gazing appreciatively at what was undoubtedly a successful party.

'We're going to bow out and leave you two lovebirds to enjoy the rest of the evening.' Callum's voice held teasing amusement as he leaned forward to kiss Irene.

'Oh, must you?'

'Duty calls, I'm afraid. I'm on emergency call after midnight.'

Alex grinned as he kissed Holly. 'One of these days we must have a long chat.'

She smiled. 'I'm glad you're feeling better. I hope you'll soon be back, working at the practice.'

He chuckled. 'One thing I've come to realise these past few weeks. I'm dispensable, and I find I don't mind a bit. In fact, I quite like the idea of retiring and living a nice quiet life, especially when I know I can hand over to someone like yourself.'

Holly felt a pang of alarm, but there was scarcely time for it to register before Callum was patting Irene's arm.

'We'll collect our coats on our way out. That way you won't need to abandon your other guests.'

It was all so smoothly managed that before she knew it, Holly found herself seated in Callum's car and the engine was purring into life.

'It was a good party,' Callum said after a few moments.

'Yes.' Good because he had met Sarah again? She closed her eyes, resting her head back against the seat. Suddenly she felt very tired. Not only tired but confused. Until a few weeks ago her life had seemed simple. Now suddenly it was full of complications.

The car came to a halt and Callum switched off the engine. It wasn't until she gazed out of the window at the unlit, unwelcoming darkness of her cottage that she even realised she was home.

Without even being aware of it, she sighed. 'Well, goodnight, and thank you...' She fumbled with the seat belt. Callum freed it for her. His arm brushed against hers, setting her heart thudding from the brief contact.

'It's late,' she muttered hoarsely, lifting her gaze to his face.

'Holly, wait.' He forestalled her attempt to open the car door as he reached across. She tried to move away but his hands were on her shoulders. His expression was shuttered, his features in shadow. 'Don't go.' His voice was uneven as his fingers stroked the silken mane of her hair.

'Please, don't,' she protested weakly. 'This isn't fair. I can't think straight.' The only thing she did know for sure was that she should put a stop to this now, while there was still time.

He leaned forward, drawing her towards him. 'Holly, I want you,' he said huskily. 'I think you want me.'

'No! It isn't true.' She turned away, but he reached for her, his hands gripping her shoulders and tugging her towards him.

'No!' She dragged her mouth away from the delicious torment he was inflicting. Her senses felt drugged. She wasn't even aware of her fingers having made contact with the warm, silky smoothness of his skin beneath his shirt until she had tried to draw away.

Her head was swimming as she tried to distance herself from him, only to feel his hands, stroking her arms, shifting to glide down the sensitive curve of her spine.

'I need you,' he said thickly. His hands ran gently through her hair, moved to her shoulders, followed the curve of her breasts, sending tremors of excitement down her spine. 'Why deny it, Holly? What is there to think about? You want me as much as I want you. You're only kidding yourself if you think otherwise.'

It wasn't true. She wouldn't let it be true. She shook her head, pushing weakly against him.

'You can lie to yourself if you want to,' he said huskily, 'but not to me, Holly. No one could respond as you do in my arms and not feel something. I can feel the way you tremble.'

'That's…that's because I don't want you to touch me.'

'You can't run away for ever, Holly,' he muttered harshly. 'Sooner or later you're going to have to let go—let the *past* go. There's a whole new future waiting out there. All you have to do is reach out. It's yours for the taking.'

'No.' Her fingers dug into the fine fabric of his shirt, feeling the powerful muscle beneath. Yes, she wanted him, but she had been down this road before, and it only led to pain. She was afraid…afraid to let go…to love again.

Love. The realisation shocked her. Was this really love? If so it seemed to bear no comparison to what she had felt for Tony.

She shook her head as a feeling of panic rose, threatening to engulf her. She had thought herself in love once before, and it had brought nothing but grief. She had vowed then that she would never go through that again.

What she was feeling now couldn't be love, she tried to tell herself. Callum McLoud had come into her life when she was still vulnerable, that was all. He had made her aware of sensations and emotions which she had never experienced before, not even with Tony. He hadn't ever said he loved her. Needed, yes. Wanted. But love… Was it any wonder she felt confused—way out of her depth?

'What are you so afraid of, Holly?' Callum's breath fanned gently against her cheek.

'Nothing. I don't know what you mean. I must go… It's late.'

'You must know I'd never do anything to hurt you. I want you, Holly. I need you in my life.'

'I…I know,' she said raggedly.

'Did you love your husband so much that you're not prepared ever to let anyone else take his place? Is that it?'

'You don't understand. Please, let me go.'

'I *want* to understand.' He held her firmly, cradled her against the hardness of his body. 'Tell me, Holly. Don't shut me out. Tell me what happened. Let me share it with you.'

'I… I can't.' She tried again to pull away but his grip merely tightened. She thought about fighting him and knew it would be futile.

'We met at the hospital where I was training,' she said thickly. 'Tony was a junior registrar.' She swallowed hard. 'We first met socially at a party, and things sort of developed from there.'

Her words were muffled as Callum drew her towards him, resting her head on his chest, his fingers gently stroking her cheek.

'Go on. You worked together?'

She nodded. 'For a while. We both moved to different departments and it wasn't always easy to meet. It wasn't as if we worked sociable hours or even the same hours. But somehow we managed to be together.'

She managed a slight smile. 'Tony was popular. He had lots of friends. He was always the life and soul of the party. That was one of the things I loved about him.' She broke off, then said hoarsely, 'We fell in love. It all seemed so perfect. When he asked me to marry him I could scarcely believe it.'

She gave a choked little laugh and rubbed the dampness from her eyes, moving fretfully. Callum held her fast, his fingers gently caressing her hair.

Holly swallowed on the tightness in her throat. 'I...I suppose I was so tied up in my studies after we were married that it didn't seem to leave much time for socialising. Maybe that's why I didn't see what was happening, didn't realise... I blame myself. I sensed that Tony was getting restless but I thought once I'd qualified it would be all right. Only by then it was already too late.'

Salt tears trickled slowly down her cheeks and this time she didn't even bother to brush them away. Her voice breaking with strain, she said, 'I knew that Tony was drinking.'

She heard Callum swear softly under his breath but couldn't bring herself to look at him. 'I'm not sure when I first realised that it wasn't just a social thing, that it was becoming a problem. It happened so gradually. It was easy to tell myself that he was bored. I wanted to spend more time with him but I had my finals—'

'That was hardly your fault, Holly. Surely he didn't expect you to throw all your training away?'

She drew a shaky breath. 'If I had, maybe things would have been different.'

'You can't believe that?'

She pushed a hand through her hair. 'He started going out without me. He said...he said I was no fun any more. We...we argued more and more, about silly things. Then, one day...'

She closed her eyes. 'I'm not sure I can—'

'Tell me, Holly. All of it.'

'We argued. It was the evening before the accident. I

can't even remember what it was about. I know he was already drunk, then...' she closed her eyes briefly in pain '...he hit me.'

A spasm flickered briefly across Callum's features. 'Oh, my love.'

'I'd heard rumours that he was seeing someone else. I didn't believe it, of course. But it hurt. It made me realise just how much we'd drifted apart and I didn't seem to be able to do anything about it. I must have been so naïve,' she said on a choked sob. 'Or maybe I just didn't want to see what was happening.'

'You weren't to blame,' Callum said. 'He knew when he married you that you were going to be a doctor. Having been through it himself, he must have known what to expect.'

She eased a tear from her cheek with her finger and Callum produced a handkerchief from his jacket pocket.

'Here, use this.'

She dried her face and said raggedly, 'On the day of the accident I should have realised he'd been drinking again. But it honestly didn't occur to me, not until I realised he was beginning to drive erratically. And when I suggested he stop and pull over and let me take over at the wheel, he...he became so angry.'

Gently Callum brushed his hand against her cheek. 'You don't have to go on.'

She drew in a deep breath. 'I'm all right. This is the first time I've talked about what happened. I just—I thought if we could just talk. If I could get him to see that he had a problem, that he was drinking too much.'

She moistened her dry lips with her tongue. 'He wouldn't discuss it. He couldn't see that there was a problem. He said if I didn't like it I could always leave.'

She closed her eyes briefly. 'I thought about it. I

couldn't see any future for us, but at the back of my mind I suppose I still hoped.'

She opened her eyes to stare down at her hands. 'And then it was too late. The accident happened so quickly. The car suddenly seemed to veer off the road. I think we must have rolled down an embankment. I...I'm not sure.'

She rolled the handkerchief into a little ball. 'It seemed to go on for ever. We must finally have come to rest. I managed to crawl out of the wreckage and get to where Tony was.' Her voice faltered. 'I could see he was badly injured. There was blood everywhere.'

Her face was pale as she looked at him. 'I stood there, looking at Tony. Her voice fell to a whisper. 'I tried to move him, but I couldn't. Then, after a while, I found Tony's mobile phone and managed to call the emergency services.'

She shook her head. 'They seemed to take for ever. I think I must have passed out. By the time they got Tony out I think I already knew he wasn't going to make it.'

She looked at Callum, her eyes filled with tears. 'What sort of person, what sort of doctor, does that make me? I should have been able to do something, anything. I should have tried harder to save him.'

'Holly, you can't spend the rest of your life blaming yourself for what happened.' Callum's voice sounded rough-edged with tension. 'From what you say, he probably didn't stand a chance anyway, and you were injured yourself. What *could* you have done?'

'I've been asking myself that question for the past two years. I haven't come up with any answers. Or, at least, not one I find it easy to live with.'

Callum frowned. 'Has it never occurred to you that Tony was responsible for what happened? You didn't force him to get drunk or to drive the car that day. That was his decision.'

Gently he forced her to look at him. 'You're a good doctor, Holly. That doesn't make you immune to all the normal emotions, and what you felt *was* perfectly normal. You have to believe that. Stop blaming yourself.' He frowned. 'Are you going to be all right?'

'Yes.' Somehow she couldn't seem to stop shaking. 'I'm sorry, I didn't mean to blurt all of this out. I don't know what happened.' She sniffed quietly. 'I'm sorry I cried all over you.'

'Forget it. It doesn't matter. Call it delayed shock.'

She stared down at the handkerchief held tightly in her fist. 'Maybe you're right.' She managed a slight smile. 'I didn't realise how much tension I'd been storing up. It was like a constantly recurring nightmare. I think, after a while, I simply switched off. I felt numb. If I didn't feel anything I wouldn't hurt any more, and it became a habit.'

'Shutting yourself off doesn't help.'

'I thought I'd deal better with it on my own.' She looked at him and said hesitantly, 'I couldn't bear all the sympathy. Don't you see? It just added to my feelings of guilt—that I hadn't cried, that I hadn't done more.'

'But now you know that the reason for that guilt doesn't exist except inside your head.'

'Yes, I can see that now.' She looked at him, her eyes shimmering like bright jewels. 'It's late. I must go,' she said huskily, 'but I'm grateful to you for listening. I think maybe I have been a little mixed up. I just need time to think things through. Do you understand?'

'Yes, I understand.'

She let out a slow, tremulous breath. Suddenly she knew she couldn't leave things as they were. She had kept her emotions in cold storage for so long, imagining they were safe. What she hadn't bargained on was someone like Callum McLoud coming along to push aside all the mental barriers she had spent so much time carefully erecting.

'You were right. There *are* things we need to talk about. Look, it's just an idea, but why don't you come over to my place tomorrow evening? I'm not the world's best cook but I could fix a casserole. We could open a bottle of wine and...'

She looked at him. He wasn't making this easy. 'I thought...maybe we could eat first and then talk.'

'It's a nice idea, Holly. But I'm afraid I can't.'

'I see,' she said flatly, feeling the colour darken her cheeks as she looked at him, and with an effort managed to force a smile. 'Well, never mind. Some other time maybe?' She was fumbling with the doorhandle when his voice stopped her.

'It's not that I don't appreciate the offer. I'm afraid I won't be here. I need to go away for a few days. I'm sorry it's going to cause some inconvenience but I was rather hoping you'd cover for me tomorrow.'

She was conscious of a sudden feeling of tightness in her throat. 'Yes, of course.' She took a deep breath and managed a smile. 'It must be important.'

A spasm flickered briefly across his features. 'There are some things I need to sort out with Sarah.'

Sarah. The girl from his past. Except that it seemed she was suddenly very much a part of the present. Holly felt her heart begin to pound. She was shocked to discover that she could actually feel jealous of a girl she didn't even really know.

'Yes, of course,' she said dully. She pushed open the car door and climbed out. 'I'll see you when you get back, then.'

She let herself into the cottage and shut the door behind her, leaning her head back against the solid wood. She felt incredibly tired and more cold than she had for a very long time, and somehow she didn't think her state of mind had anything to do with memories of Tony.

CHAPTER NINE

IT WAS snowing hard when Holly drove to the practice a couple of days later. The large, feathery flakes had settled overnight and lay in pristine drifts along the narrow roads.

She had slept badly and consequently, when she finally had drifted off, had slept so heavily that she had failed to hear the alarm. In fact, she thought, stifling a yawn, if Mac hadn't come pattering into the bedroom to tug at the duvet, she would probably still be in bed now.

Her head ached and the sight of a full waiting room did nothing to improve her temper.

Pausing at the desk to pick up the morning's mail and patients' cards, she flicked through the post and frowned.

'Damn! I was expecting the results of the blood test I did on young Lachlan Forsyth a few days ago.'

'It may come in the second delivery.' Fiona glanced at the clock. 'Is it urgent?'

'Yes, it is. The sooner I know what I'm up against, the sooner I can get his treatment sorted out. Why the hell can't these people get their act together?'

Agnes looked over Holly's shoulder. 'I can phone the haematology department for the results if you like.'

'Yes... No.' Holly raked a hand through her hair, missing the look that passed between the two women. 'When is Lachlan due to come in and see me again?'

Fiona flipped through the pages of the diary. 'Not until later in the week.'

'Oh, well, I suppose it can wait another day or so. But if it isn't here by tomorrow...'

'Don't worry. I'll start chasing them. Oh, by the way,

there was a message for you.' Fiona handed her a piece of paper, her face suddenly solemn. 'It's about David Galbraith. It's not good news, is it?'

Holly read the few words, sighed and shook her head. 'No, I'm afraid it's not.' She thought about Callum. 'Were there any other messages?'

Fiona checked and smiled. 'No. It must be your lucky day.'

No news of when Callum expected to be back, then. She hadn't realised quite how desperately she missed hearing his voice, how much she wanted to talk to him, and she was unprepared for the intense surge of disappointment that swept over her.

Then common sense took over. What was there to say? He was busy, spending his days—and probably nights—with Sarah, and the possibility that their one-time love might have been rekindled made her throat tighten painfully.

Better to put her mind to other matters. Holly sighed as the door opened, letting in a waft of cold air, and a harassed-looking young mum with a fretful toddler came into Reception.

'I'd better get on before we have a mutiny on our hands.'

'It's always like this in the run-up to the Christmas holidays. Everyone wants to be fit for the duration so no one takes any chances.' Agnes's smile became a look of concern as she followed Holly along the corridor. 'Do you feel all right? You're looking a bit peaky this morning.'

'No, as a matter of fact, I've got a splitting headache.'

'Oh, dear. Would you like me to make you a nice cup of coffee before you start surgery?'

'You're an angel.' Holly gave a slight grin of apology. 'I don't suppose you could find a couple of aspirins as well?'

'I'll do that. Oh, by the way, is there any news of Joan McGiver?'

'The lady who had the subarachnoid haemorrhage? Yes, as a matter of fact, I phoned the hospital last night. It'll be a long, slow process, but she's going to be all right.'

'Oh, well, thank heaven for that.'

Why was it, Holly wondered as she rang the bell an hour later, that when she was having a bad day anyway, things which would normally have been straightforward turned into something of a nightmare?

Rory McAllister was an overweight, ruddy-complexioned, sixty-year-old who knew his rights and wasn't about to be denied them. He eased himself into the chair and leaned forward, his fingers rapping the desk.

'I had an appointment with the other doctor.'

'Yes, Mr McAllister. Unfortunately, Dr McLoud has been called away—'

'Well, it's not good enough, messing folk around.'

'No, I realise it's very upsetting for you, but I'm afraid, on this occasion, it was unavoidable. Dr McLoud will be back in a couple of days. In the meantime, perhaps I can help?'

'Well, someone had better do something and quick about it.' Rory McAllister loosened his tie. 'I've got that there divertical thinguma-jig. Had it for a while now and not a thing been done about it.'

Holly studied her notes, trying to hide her confusion. 'Mr McAllister, I don't quite understand... I don't see anything here...'

'Well, now, that's not so surprising, is it, when I only just discovered it for myself?'

Holly turned from the written notes to the computer, bringing up the patient's medical history on the screen. 'According to these notes, the doctor last saw you a month ago. At that time you complained of abdominal pain and constipation. You were prescribed medication.'

'Aye.' His jaw jutted aggressively as he fumbled in his pocket, producing a bottle of pills which he dropped onto the desk in front of her. 'Useless they are, useless. I took one. Peppermint sweeties. What's the good of that, then?'

'But, Mr McAllister—'

'I read all about it in the book and I know what's wrong with me. It's this divertical—'

'I think you mean diverticulitis, but—'

'Aye, that's the one. Cramp in the belly, constipation, nausea. I should be in the hospital.'

Holly's lips quivered. 'Mr McAllister, I promise you, if Dr McLoud had thought for one moment that you had anything other than constipation and indigestion, he would have arranged for the necessary tests.'

She glanced at the computer screen. 'From everything you say, I have no reason to doubt Dr McLoud's opinion.' She frowned. 'I see he recommended that you include more fibre in your diet and that you eat less fatty food.'

'And I say there's nothing wrong with three good, solid meals a day. My father was brought up that way, so was his father before him, and I—'

'Have chronic indigestion?'

Rory McAllister shuffled uncomfortably in his chair. 'A man needs some meat on his bones to set him up for the winter. There's nothing to beat an old-fashioned breakfast.'

Holly glanced up. 'How many eggs do you eat in the course of a week?'

Bushy eyebrows rose. 'No more than a dozen.'

Holly stifled a sigh. 'I gather Dr McLoud discussed with you the possibility of you losing some weight?'

'Aye, so he did, and I told him a man can't live on a few lettuce leaves.'

'Dieting doesn't mean going hungry, Mr McAllister. It

simply means eating more sensibly, changing the things you eat, cutting down on fat and things like eggs.'

She looked at him directly. 'You do realise that if you go on as you are you run a serious risk of having a heart attack?'

He looked shamefaced and she knew that he hadn't even considered the implications.

'I think it might be a good idea if you were to have a word with our nurse. She'll be able to discuss your diet with you. She'll weigh you and between you you should be able to come up with some kind of compromise. So—what do you think?'

'I suppose you're right. I'll give it a try. No promises, mind.'

As he left the room she wondered whether he would be more sensible in future and pay more attention to his health, but deep down she didn't hold out much hope.

Her head was aching by the time she had seen the last of her patients. She began tidying her desk, then straightened up, easing the tension in her muscles before reaching for her jacket and briefcase.

She was looking forward to snatching a quick cup of coffee when a knock at the door drew her attention, and she looked up to see Callum standing there.

'Am I interrupting?'

'You're back,' she said, a swift wave of pleasure hitting her at the sight of him. Then the obviousness of the statement left her feeling foolish. 'No, I'd just finished.'

'I gather things have been a bit hectic while I've been away. You seem to have coped.'

'Just about.' She shrugged herself into her jacket. 'How did the trip go?'

'Fine. It's been a while since I was last away from Glenloch. I enjoyed seeing the city for a while.'

'And Sarah?' How is she?' Somehow Holly managed to

keep her voice level as she said it, and congratulated herself on not letting her tension show. 'It must have been nice to spend some time together. You must have had a lot of catching up to do.'

'We did a lot of talking. I managed to get tickets for a show.' His mouth moved in a half-smile. 'And we did some more talking. It was good.' He nodded. 'We had a great time.'

'I'm glad.' She tried to sound as if she meant it but wasn't sure she had succeeded when his blue eyes darkened and fixed on her searchingly. She looked away quickly and reached for her mobile phone.

'What will you be doing over the Christmas break?' he asked. 'Are you going away to friends or relatives? Or staying in Glenloch?'

'I…I'm not sure. I'll probably stay here and enjoy the peace and quiet.' She dropped the mobile phone into her briefcase. 'Most of my relatives are pretty widely scattered. My parents moved to Canada about four years ago, and my brother followed them a year later.' She smiled wryly. 'I doubt if I'd make the round trip in time.'

Callum looked at her. 'You must have been lonely.'

'I was alone—it's not the same thing. So, what about you? What will you be doing?'

'I'm on call so I need to stay close to the practice. I shall visit my folks. They enjoy having company, especially at this time of year.'

'Well, have a good time,' she said.

'You, too.'

She didn't see much of him after that. When she was taking surgery he was either out on a call or taking a mother and baby clinic, and before she knew it it was Christmas Eve.

Callum left at lunchtime to visit his family, and she

missed him again because it was late by the time she returned to the practice, after making her calls. She felt cheated and more than a little depressed.

For the past eighteen months she had deliberately shut herself away for the duration of the festivities, preferring not to go through the ritual merrymaking. Yet, suddenly, as patients and the practice staff said their goodbyes and the doors were locked, she felt lost.

It came as a surprise to discover that Callum had left a gift for her, though. She found it on her desk. It was wrapped in bright Christmas foil and tied with silver ribbon. She picked it up and held it to her cheek, as though it might bring him closer.

She thought of the compact disc she had bought for him, the classical guitar music that he'd once mentioned he loved, and tried to imagine him opening it on Christmas Day.

At least the cottage was cosy, with a fire burning brightly in the hearth. She had even taken the trouble to hang a few decorations and buy a small tree, which she decorated with coloured lights.

On Christmas morning, after breakfast, she opened her presents, watched by Mac who determinedly explored every piece of abandoned wrapping paper. 'Here,' she told him, fondling his ears. 'This is for you,' and don't say I never give you anything.' She gave him a squeaky toy and he rushed around the room with it, barking excitedly.

Callum's gift was an exquisite, delicately worked gold locket. She was surprised to discover that her hands were shaking as she put it on, her fingers fumbling with the clasp.

It was beautiful. She gazed at her reflection in the mirror, watching the gold catch the light. How could he have known that it was exactly what she would have chosen for herself? If only he were here so that she could put her arms around him and thank him properly.

From Jamie there was a book of her favourite poems. Fiona and Agnes had bought her talcum powder and body lotion to match her favourite perfume, and she had been surprised to receive a small gift of delicious chocolates from Alex and Irene Douglas.

All in all, Holly thought, it was one of the loneliest Christmases she had ever spent, and it was a relief when the holiday was finally over and she was back at work.

In no time at all, Holly slipped back into the familiar routine. Shortly before the holiday she had seen a patient who had suffered a series of nasty chest infections.

His X-ray results had come through and she filed them away now, thankful that there was no sign of anything sinister. Tests showed that they were dealing with a particularly nasty infection, which wasn't helped by the fact that the patient seemed to have a resistance to certain antibiotics.

But at least, now that she knew what she was up against, it should clear up soon enough with the new prescription she had given him.

Janet Carlisle was the last of her appointments and Holly could see, from the way she supported her right hand, that it was causing her a considerable amount of discomfort.

'What have you been doing to yourself?' Holly murmured, glancing at the notes on her screen.

'That's the annoying thing. I don't remember doing anything in particular,' Janet answered. 'I just started getting this weird tingling sensation in my hand. Sometimes it feels quite numb. It's quite frightening.'

'Yes, I'm sure it must be.' Holly rose to her feet, coming round the desk to make a gentle examination. 'Is your hand actually painful?'

'Oh, aye, especially at night. I get this sharp pain. It seems to shoot from my wrist up my arm.'

Holly frowned. 'And where exactly do you get the tingling sensation?'

The woman indicated her thumb and first three fingers. 'I've never had anything like it before, Doctor. It's a real nuisance, especially as I'm right-handed.'

Holly nodded. 'Yes, I imagine it must be. Can you make a fist for me?'

'Not very well,' Janet said, grimacing as she made an effort to do as Holly had asked.

'Never mind. Don't force it if it hurts,' Holly told her. She returned to her seat and rechecked the information on her computer screen. 'I see you've had problems in the past with mild arthritis in your elbow and shoulder.'

'Aye, that's right. Dr Douglas gave me an anti-inflammatory drug, I think he said. Why? Do you think this could be the same thing?'

'It's possible. What you've got is a condition called carpal tunnel syndrome.'

'And it can be caused by arthritis?'

'That's certainly one of the causes,' Holly said. 'It affects the median nerve at the wrist joint and involves the tendons and blood vessels in the hand. Sometimes it can be caused by doing work that requires a particularly strong wrist or hand action.'

'You mean, like typing or word processing?'

'Well, it could be if you weren't used to it or if you were doing repetitive work over long periods at a time.' She smiled. 'Is that what's happened?'

Janet gave a slight laugh. 'I hadn't even thought about it but, now you mention it, I did go back to college a couple of months ago. I'm thinking of going back to work now that the kids are older. I thought I'd better polish up on my office management skills—you know, practise the typing and word processing.'

'Well, that could certainly do it.'

Janet looked worried. 'This doesn't mean I have to give up on the word processing, does it?'

Holly smiled. 'Perhaps you could cut down the amount of time you spend at the keyboard. I can give you an anti-inflammatory drug which should help.'

'Well, that will be a relief.'

Holly tapped out a prescription and printed it. 'If you find the pain is particularly bad, try shaking your hands or dangling your arms. Let's see how it goes, and come and see me again in a couple of weeks.'

Janet went out and Holly, having tidied her desk, made her way to the staffroom and poured herself some coffee.

'Now, that looks like a good idea.' Callum came into the room and reached for a cup.

'You startled me!' Holly dropped the biscuit she had been holding. 'I wasn't expecting to see you today.'

'No, well, I shouldn't be here. I just came in to collect some notes and to chase up the results of a blood test.' He spooned sugar into his cup. 'Did you have a good holiday?'

'It was quiet but nice. At least I managed to relax.' She smiled. 'I'm glad I've seen you. I wanted to thank you for my Christmas present. The locket is beautiful. You shouldn't have, but I appreciate it.' She flirted briefly with the idea of flinging her arms around him and kissing him, but thought better of it.

'I'm glad you liked it.' He drained his coffee. 'I played my CD almost non-stop Christmas morning. Drove my grandparents mad.'

She laughed, and he said, 'So why were you looking so serious a few minutes ago?'

'Oh, you know, probably post-holiday blues. Getting back into a routine.'

'I would have thought you'd be used to that by now.' He studied her thoughtfully. 'Is something bothering you?'

Apart from the fact that he was standing so close that she only had to reach out to touch him? she thought wildly. She sighed. 'As a matter of fact, I *was* feeling a bit down. I had a message this morning about David Galbraith.'

Callum frowned. 'The patient with suspected prostate cancer?'

'Mmm. It was confirmed before Christmas. I'm afraid it was pretty well advanced. I heard today that he's in a bad way.' She pulled a wry face. 'I know I shouldn't let it get to me, but it does. Some doctors seem to get used to it. I never could.'

'If it did get easier I'd begin to be seriously worried that I was in the wrong job,' he said softly. 'For what it's worth, I think we just have to learn to live with it. It's part of the job and we don't help the patients by letting our emotions get in the way.'

'I'm sure you're right.' She sipped at her coffee as she leaned back against the table, enjoying the comfort of his presence. He was solid and very real and suddenly she was very glad he was there.

She thought of the moments she had spent in his arms and wished he would hold her now—that they could recapture those feelings. She stared at him, and then wished she hadn't as her eyes encountered his mouth, firm and attractive and far too much of a threat to her peace of mind.

'Holly stirred wearily. 'Well, I suppose I'd better make a move.'

'It's your half-day off, isn't it?'

'What? Oh, yes.'

Callum returned his empty cup to the tray. 'I've a couple of calls to make, but I should be finished in about an hour.

I was wondering, would you like to go for a walk? I know it's freezing hard and it will be dark early, but we could wrap up warm. Unless you've something else arranged…?'

'No.' Her heart gave a tiny, unaccustomed jerk. 'I'd love to go for a walk.'

'Fine. I'll call for you. We could take Mac with us if you like.'

She did like. All of it. Very much!

True to his word, just over an hour later Callum arrived at the cottage. He had changed out of his formal suit and was casually dressed in denim jeans and a thick, black sweatshirt. Holly was glad that she'd chosen to wear something similar, topping black ski pants with a soft, brushed cotton shirt beneath an Arran sweater.

Walking across the fields later that afternoon, with Mac romping excitedly at their heels, it was crisp and cold but invigorating. The sky was grey, giving a promise of more snow to come. The branches of the trees were bare and glittering with frost. In less than an hour it would be dark.

At any other time, with anyone else, this would seem like utter madness, Holly thought. But here and now it felt right and, given the choice, she wouldn't want to be anywhere else in the world.

They stood on the brow of a hill, their breath fanning white into the air as they watched the daylight slowly fade. Callum looked at her, a smile curving his mouth.

'Your nose is red.' He put his arm around her, drawing her close to him, his warm, solid frame protecting her against the icy wind. 'Better?'

'Mmm.' She chafed her hands, shivering not only from the cold.

'It's freezing again. I don't want you catching pneumonia again. Perhaps we should go back?'

'Oh, no! No, honestly, I love it out here. It's beautiful,

isn't it?' Suddenly she couldn't bear the thought of putting an end to what had been a perfect afternoon.

'Yes, it is.'

He held her close and she rested her head on his shoulder, feeling the warmth of him. For the first time in years she felt truly at peace with herself. She felt safe and secure. If only there was some way of making time stand still; if she could capture this moment and hold it for ever.

'I think we should go back to the car,' he said reluctantly a while later. 'It's going to be dark soon and we're in for some more snow.'

They stopped off at a small teashop, where they sat in front of a blazing log fire, drinking tea and eating hot, buttered scones. They were the only customers.

Holly wondered whether he had ever done this with Sarah. The thought left her feeling vaguely depressed but she did her best to swamp it, watching as Callum laughed aloud when Mac came to lay at his feet, his head on his paws, his soulful eyes watching hopefully for a morsel of scone to come his way.

'Don't be fooled by him.' Holly grinned. 'You'd think he hadn't been fed for a week.'

Watching Callum, Holly felt a surge of affection welling up inside her. He was a good man, gentle and caring in a way that Tony, she realised now, had never been. The thought made her throat ache, and brought a strangely hollow feeling to her stomach.

Suddenly she was filled with self-doubt. Callum was right—she saw that now. She had tried to fight it, to tell herself that there wasn't room in her life for another man. But already in her life she had made one bad mistake and maybe she could no longer rely on her instincts.

There seemed to be no defence against this man who had forced her to see that she *could* love again. The shock of the admission made her senses reel. She was in love with Callum McLoud.

A smile fleetingly touched her lips. It faded as Kate Forbes, the owner of the teashop, came to ask if they would like more tea, and jerked her attention back to the present.

A rush of heat flooded Holly's cheeks, and she turned away quickly, aware of Callum's sidelong glance.

Thinking that way was sheer folly, she silently berated herself. There was no possible future in it. Callum liked her well enough. He found her physically attractive and she knew that he would enjoy being her lover.

But that was all there was to it. It had to be. After all, there was Sarah. He had loved and lost her once. Now that she had walked back into his life, it wasn't likely that he was going to risk losing her for a second time, was it?

CHAPTER TEN

JANUARY arrived, cold but in a surprisingly amiable mood.

At the practice, the new year also started peacefully as patients and staff alike settled back into the familiar routine.

One of Holly's first patients was Vera Robertson, a sixty-year-old who looked pale and nervous as she sat in the chair.

'I saw Dr Nichols a few weeks ago. he took my blood pressure and said it was too high and that I should come back to see him after the holiday.' She glanced at the door. 'I didn't realise it was his day off.'

'No, well, it isn't usually, but he took a day's leave to visit his parents.' Holly smiled. 'His father isn't feeling too well.' She glanced at the written notes and frowned. 'Yes, I see it was rather high, wasn't it? Do you suffer from headaches?'

'No, not really.'

'Let's just take your blood pressure again now. You never know, it may have calmed down a little over the holiday.'

Holly reached for her sphygmomanometer and carried out the simple procedure. 'Yes, well, it is still higher than I'd like to see it.'

Seating herself at the desk again, she brought up the patient's previous history on the computer screen. 'I see you've had your blood pressure checked several times over the past few months, and the readings have always been on the high side, haven't they?'

'But I feel fine.'

146

Holly gave a wry smile. 'Unfortunately that's often the case with high blood pressure. There may not be any symptoms.'

'So does that mean we don't need to do anything about it?'

'I'm afraid not. Unfortunately if it isn't treated it can lead to strokes or heart attacks and sometimes kidney failure,' Holly said. 'So, looking at the reading today, I think we really need to do something about it to bring it under control.'

'It…it won't mean an operation, or having to go into hospital, will it?'

Holly smiled reassuringly. 'No, nothing like that. What I will do is start you on a course of tablets. We'll begin with a very mild dose and see how you get on with those. You'll need to take one tablet a day. Hopefully they should bring your blood pressure under control.'

'You mean, that's all there is to it?'

'Ah, not quite. I'm afraid we'll need to see you on a regular basis to check your pressure, and I'll arrange for you to have a couple of blood tests.'

The woman looked alarmed. 'Blood tests? But why?'

Holly smiled. 'It's really nothing to worry about. High blood pressure can be caused by a number of different things. In some cases it is hereditary. In others it could be caused by diabetes. 'Not,' she added hastily, 'that I have any reason to suppose you have diabetes, but we need to eliminate it as a possibility.'

She glanced at the computer screen. 'High blood pressure is also sometimes an indicator that you might have a high cholesterol level, too, so we need to check it out.'

'And if it is high?'

Holly smiled. 'Well, if it is, sometimes it's simply a matter of making adjustments to your diet. To the amount of saturated fats you eat. Or, in some cases, you may need

tablets to bring the level down. But let's cross that bridge
if and when we come to it.'

She handed the woman a prescription. 'If you see the
nurse on your way out, she'll probably be able to do the
blood tests now.'

She rose to her feet and Vera Robertson followed suit.

'See how you get on with the tablets. If you're at all
worried come back and see me. I shall need to see you in
any case in a couple of months' time to give you a repeat
prescription. In the meantime, we should have the results
of the blood tests in about a week.'

Vera Robertson pulled a face. 'I'm not so keen on nee-
dles.'

'I know the feeling but, I promise you, our nurse has a
magic touch. You'll hardly feel a thing.'

Holly smiled and watched her leave the room. All in all
it was a quiet morning. Two hours later she had seen her
last patient and it left her a little time to go over the notes
she had made for the first of the prostate cancer advisory
meetings arranged for the following week.

She had spoken to Jamie. They had both consulted their
diaries and he wanted to take her out to dinner in a couple
of days' time so that they could talk through the final plans
for the forthcoming evening.

So far she was pleased with the way things were going.
She had decided that it would be best to keep the whole
thing as informal as possible, with a short introductory
talk, followed by a brief film show and a question-and-
answer session.

All Holly had to do now was to decide on what refreshments to offer. She had debated briefly with herself on
whether, in fact, to provide more than tea or coffee, and
had finally decided that, as some of those participating
might bring partners, offering refreshments would be a
good opportunity to get people to relax and mingle.

Some light snacks to nibble on, and perhaps fruit juice or wine? She was reaching for her notepad when there was a knock at the door and Fiona came in. The girl looked worried.

'Is anything wrong?' Holly asked.

'It's… Irene Douglas rang a few minutes ago. It's Alex. He's not feeling too well. She's obviously worried about him.'

Her face draining of colour, Holly was out of her chair and heading for the door before the girl could finish speaking. 'I'll go straight over there.'

In the corridor she almost collided with Callum as the door of the room opposite burst open. Other than in passing, she hadn't seen him for a few days. Somehow careful avoidance had seemed the best policy and she was unprepared as an indefinable sense of longing surged through her.

'Callum! I didn't know you were in.'

'I'm not, officially. I was just catching up on some paperwork.' He looked at her and frowned. 'What's happened?'

'It's Alex.'

'Alex?'

'Irene just phoned,' Holly said grimly. 'It seems he's not feeling too well. I'm just on my way over there.'

'Did she say what was wrong?'

Fiona shook her head. 'She just said she's worried about him. Her son and daughter-in-law are away and she asked if someone go and take a look at him.'

'Then she must have good reason. Irene isn't the sort of woman who panics easily.'

Holly said, 'I'm on my way there now.' She looked at him. 'Will you come? He knows you.'

'I'll be with you in a few seconds—let me just grab my

bag. We can take your car. Mine is still loaded with equipment.'

The drive from the practice to the Douglases' house took barely ten minutes. As they came to a halt on the gravel drive, the door was already open and Irene Douglas came to meet them.

'Thank you for coming so quickly. I didn't know what to do.'

'How is he?'

'Cross! He says I shouldn't have called you, that I'm wasting your time.'

'Well, let's hope he's right. Where is he?'

'Through here.'

Callum didn't waste any time. He headed straight for the sitting room. Holly followed blindly, mentally steeling herself for what they might find.

Alex Douglas was sitting in a chair, his eyes closed as he rested his head back against a cushion. He looked pale and his skin was clammy. His eyelids fluttered open and he managed a smile as they reached him.

'I'm so sorry about this. I feel so stupid. I didn't want Irene to bother you.'

'She did the right thing. The trouble with some people is they're too stubborn for their own good.'

Callum was a man of speedy reflexes. The reassuring smile was an added bonus, Holly thought as, with calm, unhurried movements, he knelt beside the man to begin making a gentle examination.

'Do you have any pain anywhere?'

Alex's hand fluttered vaguely towards his chest. 'Some. Not bad. Just a damned nuisance.' He coughed.

Callum reached for his stethoscope, applying it to the man's chest. 'Any problems with the breathing?'

Alex nodded. 'For a few days now. Bit wheezy.'

'Alex, why on earth didn't you tell me?' Irene Douglas chided as she reached for his hand.

'It's nothing. I didn't want you fussing and worrying.'

Holly saw Callum's lips tighten fractionally as he concentrated on his examination. A few seconds later he straightened up. 'Why didn't you call the surgery, Alex? You know someone would have come to see you. Dammit! It doesn't have to be an emergency before you get in touch.'

'Didn't want to be any trouble.'

'You have a temperature—I suppose you know that?'

'I'll take your word for it.'

'Any pain in your arms?'

'Are you asking *me*, in the nicest possible way, if it's another heart attack?'

Holly glanced at Irene. Tears glistened faintly behind the older woman's lashes. 'You're a stubborn old fool, Alex Douglas.'

'So I've been told.' Smiling slightly, he reached up to clasp his wife's hand. 'I'm sorry to be such a bother to you.'

'Oh, away with you.'

Callum drew up a chair and sat down. 'Well, if it's any consolation I don't think it is another heart attack.'

Holly heard Irene Douglas's soft intake of breath.

'I dare say you've been overdoing things.' Callum gave a wry smile. 'You never were one to take advice, were you, Alex?' He coiled the stethoscope, dropping it into his briefcase. 'What you've got is a chest infection. I'll give you some antibiotics. Hopefully you should start to feel better in a couple of days.'

Irene sniffed hard. 'I think what we all need is a nice cup of tea. I'll away and switch on the kettle.'

Callum wrote out a prescription, placing it on the nearby table. 'You know you're going to have to take things a bit

more easily for a while, Alex? Sensible exercise after a
heart attack is one thing, but I get the impression you
haven't altogether been sensible.' Callum's mouth firmed.
'I mean it, Alex. Ease up.'

'Why not enjoy the rest while you can?' Holly urged,
smiling. 'A few more weeks and you'd be raring to go.'

'Aye, it's a nice thought.' Alex smiled. 'But if there's
one thing I've had of late, it's time. Believe me, the nov-
elty wears off.'

'So why not take a holiday?' Callum shifted his briefcase from the table to make room for the laden teatray
Irene carried through from the kitchen.

'Holiday?' She gave a laugh as she handed round the
tea. 'I sometimes think he's forgotten the meaning of the
word. We've talked about taking a wee cruise. But that's
as far as it ever gets—talk. There always seems to be
something more important.'

'So why not think about it now?' Holly sipped at her
tea. 'Why not just pick up the phone and call your nearest
travel agent? Imagine it…' Smiling, she glanced through
the window at the snow-laden sky. 'You could swap all
this for some sun. I know what I'd do, given the choice.'

Irene Douglas glanced at her husband. 'Well?'

'Well, what?'

'I'm waiting for the excuse.'

Alex gazed thoughtfully into his teacup, before looking
at her. 'You know, I can't think of a single one.'

Irene made a pretence at fainting. 'I don't believe it!
He's agreeing to take a real holiday.' She was on her feet
and heading for the door.

'Where are you going, woman? Your tea's going cold.'

'I'm away to phone the travel agent now, before you
have time to change your mind.'

It was only later, after she found herself being ushered
into the car, that Holly realised she had been relieved of

her keys and was sitting in the passenger seat while Callum drove. It also occurred to her that she was happy to let him take charge.

Closing her eyes, she shivered as weariness seemed suddenly to set in. The Douglases were a nice couple. She found herself enjoying their quiet certainty in each other. The kind of confidence that comes from a relationship built up over many years. But, then, they were amongst the lucky ones.

The car drew to a halt and she sat gazing out of the window, only then noticing that they were at Callum's house, not at the cottage. But, of course, she realised, it made sense, as he had left his own car behind at the surgery.

She stirred reluctantly. Suddenly the prospect of going back to the empty cottage, alone, seemed less than inviting.

'Come in for a drink. I don't know about you,' Callum said, 'but I need one, even if it's only coffee, and I hate drinking alone.'

'Mrs Clarke...'

'Is away to her sisters in Edinburgh for a few days.' His mouth relaxed into a smile. 'Don't worry, Holly, you're quite safe—unless you'd rather be otherwise,' he said gruffly.

Put like that, how could she refuse?

She followed him into the house through to the kitchen, where Callum flipped the switch on the electric percolator, before reaching for mugs from a shelf.

'Why don't you go into the sitting room and make yourself comfortable? I just want to check the answering machine for messages. I'll bring the tray through as soon as the coffee's ready.'

Left to her own devices, Holly wandered through to the sitting room. A fire had burned low in the hearth. Without thinking, she reached for a poker and stirred the embers

back to life, before adding a log from the nearby box.
Within seconds the fire crackled into life.

She moved to sit in one of the large armchairs. There
was something almost hypnotic about a real fire, watching
the flames, orange, red and blue, lick around the dry wood.

It felt strange, safe, secure, being back here. There was
a feeling almost of having come home. Except, she reminded herself dully, this could never be home, not for
her. For Sarah, maybe.

She sighed without even being aware of it.

'Sorry about that. I had to make a call.'

She looked up to see Callum, standing in the doorway.
He was studying her so intently that she rose quickly.

'I'm sorry, I made myself comfortable.' She ran a hand
awkwardly through her hair. There was something disturb-
ingly arousing about him as he stood with the halllight
behind him, the dark trousers hugging his hips, his eyes
appearing a deeper blue than ever.

She let her gaze fall warily. 'Do you need any help out
there?'

He shook his head. 'Coffee's almost ready. Everything's
under control.'

Except my heart, she thought wildly. The effect of the
lamplight, the fire, his nearness, were creating an intensity
of sexual awareness that took her breath away. It was a
heady, intoxicating sensation.

She gave a slight laugh. 'I feel guilty. I'm not used to
being waited on.'

'Why not just relax and enjoy it? One way and another
it's been quite a day, for both of us.' Callum looked at her
searchingly. 'Come here,' he said softly, holding out his
arms to her. 'You look exhausted.'

'As bad as that?' she murmured, but she went anyway,
allowing him to fold her in his arms and soothe away the

tensions of the day. It felt good, and right. Like…coming home.

She couldn't have said when the comforting became something more than that, but as she raised her head to look at him he groaned softly and then, suddenly, his mouth was making teasing advances against her lips, her throat, the lobes of her ears and back to her shamelessly unresisting mouth, claiming it with a determination that left them both breathless.

She responded with a ferocity that matched his own, driven by a raw kind of hunger. Callum raised his head briefly, breathing hard as he looked at her before drawing her to him again.

'I've wanted to do that for so long,' he muttered roughly against her hair. 'When I'm not with you I tell myself I won't rush things, but the moment I see you all my good intentions seem to fly out of the window. Even at Alex's place, when I know I should have been concentrating on other things, I wanted to take you in my arms.'

'I'm glad you were there,' she whispered, when she could breathe again. 'I know how much they both mean to you. When the call came through I expected the worst, that it might be another heart attack, and I wasn't sure I could handle the responsibility if anything went wrong.'

'You would have coped.' His hands moved over her, shaping her slenderness, rousing her to a peak of desperation.

She closed her eyes, moaning softly as a whole gamut of emotions ran through her.

'I want you, Holly.' His breath seemed to catch shakily in his throat. 'Have you any idea what it's doing to me, having you so close? I need you, Holly. I want to make love to you.'

'I know,' she said weakly. She rocked on her feet, her senses seeming drugged as she looked up at him.

'I won't do anything to hurt you.' His fingers were at the buttons of her blouse.

She drew a shuddering breath as his hand moved to caress her breast, shocked as the taut nipple flowered in instant response. The effect of his touch was even more potent than she had ever imagined it could be.

'I didn't intend rushing things,' he said huskily. 'I'm not sure I can stick to that. I need you, Holly.'

'I know.'

He drew a harsh breath as he looked at her for a long moment, then pulled her roughly towards him. 'Stay with me tonight, Holly.'

His hands were moving over her body, rousing her again. She closed her eyes, moaning softly.

'This is completely crazy.'

'I know,' he breathed as he slid her blouse over her shoulders.

Her mobile phone rang. Involuntarily she stiffened.

'Ignore it,' he rasped.

'I can't. I'm on emergency call.' She detached herself slowly from his arms.

He cursed softly under his breath as she moved away to take the call.

'Yes, Dr Hunter speaking.' She reached up to press her fingers against Callum's marauding lips. 'Yes, and she has a temperature? Right, I'll be there in about fifteen minutes.' She fumbled to restore her blouse to order. 'I have to go, Callum.'

He gave a short, unsteady laugh. 'Wrong time, wrong place,' he muttered. 'It's your morning off tomorrow, and I have a clinic in the afternoon. Look, perhaps I can drop by your place in the evening? We can talk—over a glass of wine, maybe?'

Holly shook her head. 'I promised I'd call in at the hospital to see Joan McGiver.'

'The evening after that?'

'I can't.' She ran her tongue over her lower lip. 'I'm having dinner with Jamie. The meeting is looming and we still need to discuss the programme. We need to—'

'That's all right. You don't need to explain.'

'But I—'

'It doesn't matter, Holly,' he said dismissively. 'It was just a passing thought. I dare say we'll see each other around.'

She shivered, sensing him moving away, as if an invisible barrier had come down between them. 'At the weekend maybe?'

'I've arranged to see Sarah. She's moving out of her flat into a new place. I told her I'd help ferry a few things for her.'

He glanced swiftly at his watch. 'You'd better go. We can't have the patients complaining they've been kept waiting.'

His face had taken on a shuttered look, and Holly knew that whatever she said the moment had been lost. He was no longer in a mood to listen.

Perhaps it was just as well, she thought dismally. As he'd said, it had just been a passing thought. All right, so he had kissed her but it had been no more than a comforting gesture that had run rapidly out of control.

Maybe it was as well things had been called to a halt. It was probably best if she kept out of his way, she decided, sighing heavily as moments later she drove away from the cottage.

The last thing she wanted was to be second-best, a momentary consolation prize while he sorted out his feelings for the girl from his past.

Things were in a state of near chaos over the following week, as Agnes had gone off sick with pharyngitis and

Kirsty was off with flu.

Jamie had taken a couple of long overdue leave days to spend some time with his sister and her family, over on a surprise visit from Australia where they lived, and Callum was away at a medical conference so that no one had been in touch with him.

On top of that, their arrangement to take on a locum during the particularly busy period had broken down, and Holly decided that the only thing to be done was to add Jamie's patients to her list over the next few days and take on some of his calls.

If she had imagined Callum might be happy about her initiative, she soon discovered that she couldn't have been more wrong.

'What the devil's going on here?' he demanded tersely, coming in late one day to find her still working her way through her list of evening appointments.

'We've been busy,' she told him, hunting through the shelves for an elusive package of notes. And to think she had actually been missing this man! 'You know what it's like at this time of year. We're seeing a lot of patients with flu symptoms and coughs.'

'I don't need you to tell me what kind of pressures we're up against. It isn't the point. We also have a system that's supposed to work perfectly well, without you needing to take on everyone else's job.'

His glance raked her. 'Look at yourself. You're as pale as a ghost and look as if you haven't slept for a week.'

'Thanks a lot,' she returned with dry sarcasm. 'I wasn't looking for a sympathy vote. It just so happens that I was out on an emergency call last night and I've taken a couple of surgeries today.'

She turned to the desk to check the appointments book.

'It's hardly surprising if I look a little pale, but it's no big deal.'

'I've heard about the extra hours you've been putting in. You've no business working to that extent. It isn't fair to you and it certainly isn't fair to the patients.'

She stiffened defensively. 'How dare you accuse me of giving less than my best to my patients?'

'I'll accuse you of anything I like, if it happens to be true,' he said sharply. 'How do you expect to function properly on practically no sleep and working the sort of ridiculous hours you've been putting in—least of all you.'

Her hackles rose. 'What do you mean—least of all me?'

'It isn't so very long ago since you were quite seriously ill,' he bit out. 'The last thing you need is to get overtired and run down.'

She glowered at him. 'Are you saying I'm not capable of doing my job?'

'I wouldn't dream of it,' he said coolly. 'But the operative word is your job. That doesn't mean taking on everyone else's work. What happened to the locum we'd arranged to come in?'

'He was taken ill at the last minute. It's hardly surprising. There have been so many cases of flu, people going down like flies...'

'Why wasn't I informed about the change of plans?'

She gave a slight laugh. 'What good would it have done? Besides, I understood that Agnes did keep you in touch with what was going on.'

'I could have made other arrangements for some temporary help if I'd known what was happening,' he said harshly. 'I was told everything was under control.'

'Which it was. You can hardly blame Agnes or Fiona for telling you what they thought to be true. Everyone is under pressure.'

'Can't I? Well, I have to disagree.' Callum stormed out

of the room and headed through to Reception. Holly sighed heavily. She thought he was behaving unreasonably, but now obviously wasn't a good time to debate the issue.

Instead, she rang the bell for her next patient. As she waited she wondered what had happened to make him so angry. Perhaps things weren't going so well between him and Sarah. After all, their relationship had foundered once before, and a lot of water had gone under the bridge since then.

Maybe picking up the pieces hadn't been quite as simple as they had imagined. Somehow Holly couldn't find it in her to feel sorry about that.

With an effort, she managed to drag her thoughts back to her work. She stared at the screen, trying to familiarise herself with the notes.

Callum had no right to suggest that she wasn't giving her best to her patients. She hadn't wanted or asked for this job, but as she had accepted the commitment she had done her best to deal with her patients' problems.

She only hoped that the prostate advisory meeting would go without a hitch. It had taken time and effort to put it together and it meant a lot to her.

If it went well, it might, hopefully, prevent a lot of people going through the kind of anguish being suffered by David Galbraith and his family right now.

Jamie was certainly on good form on the evening of the meeting when finally it arrived. If she'd had any doubts about what kind of turnout there would be, or how the audience would react to the subject of prostate cancer, her fears were soon laid to rest as Jamie quickly won them over.

He spoke knowledgeably, emphasising the positive while not glossing over the truth that, if not caught and treated in time, prostate cancer was a killer. He gave them the facts and, during the course of the evening, as she made her own contribution to the proceedings, Holly saw several couples glance at each other and reach out to hold hands.

The talk was followed by a lively question-and-answer session and, again, no punches were pulled. Afterwards there was a break for refreshments, which had been laid out in an adjoining room, and there were leaflets, offering useful advice.

'Well, I'd say it went jolly well, wouldn't you?' Jamie said, helping himself to a sausage roll and a glass of white wine after he'd handed Holly a glass. 'And the idea of providing refreshments afterwards was a positive brainwave.' He raised his glass in salute. 'Congratulations. I'd say you've got a success on your hands.'

'I couldn't have done it without you. You seemed to put over the message about checking for early signs of prostate problems and then getting help and advice quite succinctly, but without causing any panic.'

'You could have handled the evening equally well by yourself, you know.'

Holly shook her head. 'I'm sure men, most men, still feel more comfortable listening to another man.' She smiled. 'Still, the important thing is that we seem to have got the message over, and that's what counts.' She looked round the room. 'I was pleased to see that so many wives and partners turned up, too.'

Jamie grinned. 'Don't tell me, you'll be thinking up something for the ladies as well.'

'Well, why not?' She laughed. 'I know we have the Well Woman clinic, but it doesn't always have to be so formal. There still seems to be this mistaken belief that the menopause is the end of…of femininity somehow, and it isn't. It's just the beginning of a new chapter—a time to re-evaluate themselves and their lives.'

Jamie grinned again, holding up his hands in mock surrender. 'Hey, I'm on your side. We're the good guys, remember?'

'Sorry. I seem to have acquired a hobby-horse, don't I? But what's wrong with concentrating on the positive side? Women might enjoy focusing on learning how to make the best of themselves.'

'You mean girly chats about make-up?'

She slapped him playfully. 'Not just make-up. Talks on fashion, colour consultancy.' She laughed. 'I wouldn't mind a little advice myself. I seem to have got into the habit of throwing on the most sensible, convenient clothes in the morning.'

Jamie's glance slid over her appreciatively. 'Oh, I think you're doing just fine as you are.'

Holly was wearing a long-sleeved blouse of soft, silky fabric in a delicate amber colour that added warmth to her pale complexion. A loose-fitting velvet jacket and a calf-length skirt completed the outfit.

Seeing his expression, it reminded her of the recent evening they had spent together, and of how attentive he had been, and she suddenly wondered whether she had made a wise decision. She lowered her head and sipped at her drink to hide her confusion.

'The evening seems to be going very well,' Callum said, coming to stand beside her and subjecting her to a penetrating scrutiny.

'You're looking a little flushed. Is that because you're enjoying your success, or has Jamie been flirting with you again?'

Jamie looked unabashed. 'I'm just being my normal, red-blooded self. This is one beautiful, unattached young woman, Doctor—or hadn't you noticed? Too busy sighing over the delightful Sarah maybe? Well, each to his own.'

'I suggest we keep personal remarks out of this,' Callum

advised him coolly. 'Remember where we are. It wouldn't look too good if we came to blows.'

'I dare say it's the excitement. The evening went even better than we'd dared to hope,' Holly put in quickly before the conversation had a chance to get out of hand. She could see that Jamie wasn't amused by that comment, and from Callum's tone she wasn't entirely sure that he was joking.

'I hope you're not planning to drive?' Callum said. He looked at Holly. 'I have my car outside. I'll drive you home.'

'That won't be necessary,' Jamie intervened. 'I've already persuaded Holly to come back to my place for coffee. I'll make sure she gets home safely.'

Callum's narrowed glance shifted to Holly. 'In that case there's nothing more to be said. I'll see you tomorrow.' He turned to go, then stopped and said, 'Perhaps we should have a practice meeting to discuss the benefits, or otherwise, of tonight's meeting, just in case we decide to put on something similar in the future.'

His smooth return to business matters left her feeling as if a door had been slammed in her face. For a moment or two there she had allowed herself to believe he might be jealous that she was seeing another man.

She had been fooling herself, she could see that now—had been fooling herself all along. There was no future for her with Callum. Their relationship was, and always would be, strictly professional.

Maybe it was best that way, she thought as she watched him leave. It would certainly be less wearing on her nerves.

Sometimes she wished she had never ever met Callum McLoud, and knew that even that wasn't true. He had walked into her life and turned it upside down. There might not be any future in it, but there was no going back.

The fact that he wanted her didn't mean a thing—she realised that now. Wanting and loving were too entirely different things and it seemed that his love was all reserved—for Sarah.

CHAPTER ELEVEN

ANY hopes Holly might have had that Callum's mood might have improved by the following day were dashed the moment she arrived at the surgery.

The air of tension hit her even before she reached the desk.

'Yes, Doctor. I'll see to it. No...' Fiona looked up, saw Holly and pulled a wry face as she shifted the receiver away from her ear. 'Yes, I'll have the letter on your desk in five minutes.'

She replaced the receiver and sighed deeply.

'Trouble?' Holly put her briefcase down and reached for the diary.

'You could say. I don't seem to have done a thing right since I walked in the door.' Fiona gave a slight smile. 'I think I should have stayed in bed.'

'Oh, dear.' Holly glanced in the direction of Callum's door. 'Like that, is it?'

'It's not like him.' Agnes added another card to the growing pile on the desk.

'Well, all I can say it it's just as well or some of us might be looking for another job.' Defiantly, Fiona flipped the switch on the electric kettle and reached for a carton of milk. 'I don't care if it isn't time. I need a coffee.'

'Make that two.' Agnes sighed.

'Tell you what, make it three and I'll bring the aspirins.'

Holly made her way to her consulting room, pausing on the way to glance in at Callum's open door. He was busy, clearing his desk and pushing papers into his briefcase. He seemed preoccupied and scarcely glanced up as she spoke to him.

'Can you spare a minute, or is this an awkward time?'

He glanced at his watch. 'No, now is fine, if you make it quick. What's the problem?'

'Not a problem as such. I just…well, I just wanted to thank you, that's all.'

He glanced up, frowning. 'For what?'

She gave a small laugh. 'For giving your approval to last night's meeting. I appreciate it.'

'You didn't need my approval.' He glanced impatiently round the room, reached for a folder and dropped it into his briefcase.

Holly frowned. 'I think you know what I mean. I couldn't have gone ahead with it if you'd been against the idea.'

'Why would I do that?'

She sighed. He definitely wasn't making this easy. His briefcase was on the desk, with his mobile phone, keys and jacket. 'You look as if you're in a hurry,' she commented, hoping her voice sounded less shaky than she suddenly felt. 'Have you made plans for the weekend?'

She was glad it was Saturday tomorrow and that she wasn't on duty. She felt deathly tired. Nights of lying awake were getting to her and the galling thing was that hours of staring at the ceiling hadn't provided any answers, except that she knew things between herself and Callum couldn't go on as they were.

'Yes, I am, and I have,' he answered shortly, and she wondered briefly what he would say if she asked if they could put the clock back, metaphorically speaking, and start again.

'Going somewhere nice?' The moment the words were out she wished them unsaid. She didn't want to know. Some things, like Pandora's box, were best left alone.

'I'm going to Edinburgh. How about you?'

Yes, of course. Sarah. A small pain seemed to stab at her heart. 'I'm not sure yet.' With an effort she managed a smile. 'I may just take the phone off the hook, hide the alarm and sleep the clock round—Mac permitting.' She stifled a jaw-cracking yawn. 'Oh, dear, sorry.'

'Lingered over the coffee with Jamie last night, did you? You'll soon learn that you can't afford to burn the candle at both ends.'

His voice was edged with sarcasm and she stared at him, shocked by the cynicism in his tone.

'I may have been a little later than usual—'

He gave a short laugh. 'Yes, I'm sure. Not one to pass up an opportunity is our Jamie.'

His mouth twisted and Holly stiffened defensively. 'What exactly are you trying to say?' She met his gaze directly. 'Are you suggesting that I stayed out all night?'

'Didn't you?'

She couldn't believe he had said it. 'Why on earth would you think that?'

'Probably because I drove past your cottage in the early hours of this morning. One of my patients went into labour. She was due to be delivered at home but there were complications so I was called out. Your car wasn't there and I know you weren't on call.'

'I see,' she said quietly. 'So you drew the obvious conclusion—that I must have spent the night with Jamie?'

'I didn't say that.'

'But you inferred it. As a matter of fact,' she said quietly, 'I *was* on duty. Officially, Jamie should have been on call, but he stayed behind with me to help clear the hall after everyone had left. He packed up the screen and projector, and by the time we'd cleared the refreshments away it was late. I felt the least I could do, by way of thanks, was to offer to cover emergency calls for him.'

Callum said nothing, just continued to sift through his papers, quickly scrawling his signature on a couple of letters. She looked at him curiously, afraid even to hope that jealousy might have been the cause of his ill-temper.

'I thought Jamie was your friend,' she said quietly. 'Don't you think you're being unfair, especially after all the help he gave us? He didn't have to do it.'

'Don't fool yourself that it was for us, Holly. We both know it was for you.' He snapped his briefcase shut. 'Anyway, I'm not annoyed with Jamie. For the past week I've been trying to buy a special gift. The store had to order the item and promised it would be delivered within a couple of days. It didn't arrive.'

So much for the tiny spark of hope which had flickered briefly to life in her chest. Served her right for letting her imagination run riot, Holly thought.

'Is it urgent?'

'Yes, it is rather. I need to take it with me today. I've just phoned the store and they say I can pick it up now. Which means, with any luck, I can still be in Edinburgh before dark.'

'You're looking forward to seeing Sarah again.'

He shrugged himself into his jacket and dropped his mobile phone into the pocket. 'I'd originally planned to travel in the morning. She thought it might be quicker and easier tonight—less likely to be delays with the traffic.'

'Yes, well, there is that. And obviously you'll want to spend as much time together as possible,' Holly said distantly. 'When do you plan to get back?' She despised herself for feeling the need to ask.

'Some time on Monday. I'm on call then anyway.'

Otherwise he might have stayed longer. 'Well, it sounds good.' She tried to keep the dismay out of her voice. 'I'd better not keep you. You'll obviously want to get away as soon as possible,' she muttered. 'Have a lovely weekend.'

Callum followed as she headed blindly for the door.

'I'll see you Monday then.'

Her throat felt almost too tight to speak. 'Yes.'

She wished he would just go before she broke down completely. In her consulting room the phone was ringing. She moved like an automaton towards it, snatching at the receiver as if it were a lifeline.

'Holly?' Callum stood in the doorway. There was no mistaking the strain on his face. Her own emotions were so close to the surface that she wasn't sure she could trust herself to be near him without letting go.

Tell me you love me, she wanted to shout at him. Instead, she said quietly into the phone, 'Yes? Oh, Jamie. No, you caught me just in time, as a matter of fact.' Before I could make a complete fool of myself. 'I was just about to make a start on surgery.'

She gave a slight smile. 'Yes, it went very well. I enjoyed it. I think we achieved all we set out to. Yes, so did I.' She was vaguely aware of Callum turning away. She had to resist the urge to call him back, to hug him, to hold him tight.

But what could she say? Please, don't go? I love you? But, then, Sarah loved him too, and he loved Sarah, twice over.

The weekend was like a bad dream for Holly, to be got through somehow, anyhow. She deliberately kept busy in a desperate attempt to shut out thoughts of Callum and Sarah together, but somehow, no matter how hard she tried, she still couldn't rid her mind of those unhappy images.

On Saturday she took Mac for a long walk. The grass was crisp with frost, but she put on her boots, trousers, sweater and a heavy jacket and stayed determinedly out of the cottage until exhaustion and hunger finally drove them both back home.

Sunday was even more bleak as a blanket of freezing fog crept in and settled over the countryside. She spent the day inventing chores and it was almost a relief when it was time to go to work the next morning.

By lunchtime the waiting room was empty at last. Back at the cottage, Holly drank a quick cup of coffee and swallowed a couple of aspirin as she checked the messages on her answering machine. One more call to add to the list— at this rate she'd be lucky to make it back for evening surgery.

By mid-afternoon she had to switch on the car headlights, and the temperature had plummeted by several degrees.

Switching on the radio, she half-listened to the latest news bulletin. 'An accident has closed part of the motorway... Driving conditions made worse... More heavy snowfalls expected...'

Holly tried to dismiss the sudden qualm that rippled through her at the news. Callum would be home now, wouldn't he? He'd said he had to be back because he was on call, so it wasn't likely he'd be caught up in that motorway chaos. Besides, he was an excellent driver.

Climbing out of the car, she locked the door and stood for a few seconds, breathing hard as she made the trek across the farmyard. The door was opened by an anxious-looking woman of about fifty.

'Sorry it took me a while to get to you, Gladys,' Holly apologised as she stepped inside the big, stone-built house, brushing flakes of snow from her hair as she did so. 'I had a list of calls as long as your arm and the weather isn't helping.'

'Aye, and it looks as if we're in for a lot more yet. Come

away in. Will you have a cup of tea, Doctor? I just made a fresh brew.'

'I'd love to, Gladys…' Holly glanced, frowning, at her watch '…but I'd better not.' She smiled ruefully. 'Dr McLoud has been away for the weekend. He's due back for surgery but the way things are going… Anyway, you said your father isn't feeling too well?'

'That's right. He's not been so bright this past few days.'

'In what way?'

'Oh, he says he has a headache. It's not like him. I've given him aspirin but it doesn't seem to shift it.' Shedding her apron, Gladys led the way to the stairs. 'He was dozing a while ago. That's not like him either.'

'You should have called me before.'

'Oh, you know how it is. I told him I'd ring the surgery, but you know what he's like. Stubborn as a mule. When he took to his bed today I knew it was more serious. He's never been a man who liked his bed.' She pushed open the door. 'Hello, Dad. Look who's come to see you.'

'Hello, Neil. Gladys tells me you're feeling a bit out of sorts.'

The occupant of the bed struggled from beneath a mound of covers to sit up. At eighty years of age Neil Fairburn had the weathered features of someone who had lived an outdoor life.

Gladys was his only surviving family. His son had been killed in a road accident and his wife had died three years ago, all of which had strengthened the bond between father and daughter.

Gladys moved to help him sit up, and plumped the pillows behind him. She raised her voice as she said, 'I told the doctor you've got a nasty headache, Dad.'

'Aye.' He raised one frail hand, pressing it shakily to

his forehead as he turned slowly, almost gingerly, to look in Holly's direction.

She noted, as she sat on the edge of the bed, that he looked flushed. 'How long have you had the headache, Neil?'

He looked at his daughter and Gladys nodded. 'About four days. Four days it's been pretty bad, anyway.'

'Is it there all the time?'

'Not so bad when I wake up. Gets worse as the day goes on.'

Holly nodded. 'And what about when you turn your head?'

'Flashing lights.'

'Ah. I just want to check your throat and glands.' Holly made a quick but thorough examination, pressing her fingers gently in the process against the man's cheek-bones and above his eyes.

Neil Fairburn grunted.

'That's painful, is it? Well, don't worry, we'll soon sort it out and have you feeling better.'

Moving slightly away from the bed, she said, 'Well, I'm sure it's nothing serious. He's got a nasty sinus infection and it's obviously making him feel pretty rotten.'

'Dad's not one to like being poorly.'

'No, I'm sure he's not. Look, I'm going to give you a prescription for an antibiotic and some different painkillers. I think you'll find he should be feeling much better in a couple of days.'

Holly wrote out the prescription, handing it to the woman. 'It won't hurt him to stay in bed for a while, but I'd encourage him to get up tomorrow. Meanwhile, if you're at all worried, give me a call.'

It was already late when she returned to the practice, parked her car and ran through the gusting, snow-laden wind into the surgery. A peep into the waiting room sent her hurrying through to Reception.

'What on earth happened? Where is everyone?'

'Staying at home and battening down the hatches, if they've any sense.' Agnes placed a file of typed letters on the desk. 'Just as well, from the look of things out there, I'd say.'

'I wasn't sure I'd get here myself,' Fiona said, as she directed the next patient to the treatment room. 'The snow's lying pretty deep on some of the outlying roads and I heard something on the radio about an accident. It sounded pretty bad.'

Holly felt a sudden shiver pass down her spine. 'Has anyone heard from Callum yet? Shouldn't he be back by now?'

'There's probably a backlog of traffic. I expect he's caught up in it somewhere.' The phone began to ring in the office. Frowning, Agnes went to answer it.

'I'm surprised he didn't use the mobile to call in,' Fiona said, 'He usually does if he's going to be late.'

With an effort, Holly managed a smile. 'Oh, I expect he was probably just late starting back.' So why wasn't she convinced? 'Anyway, he wouldn't come that way, would he?'

'I doubt if he'd have any choice. I heard some of the minor roads are closed. The snow ploughs are out.'

'Callum's on the phone,' Agnes interjected quietly as she came through from the office. She looked at Holly. 'He asked to speak to you.'

Relief swamped Holly as she hurried to the phone, annoyed with herself now for having let her imagination run away with her.

'Callum.' Taking a deep breath, she said jokingly, 'What time do you call this? Some people will do anything to avoid taking surgery…'

'Holly, I'm sorry it's taken so long to get through to you.' His voice was deep and gratifyingly strong. 'Look, I'm not going to make it back in time for evening surgery. Can you get Jamie to cover for me? There's been an accident on the motorway.'

'Yes, I know. We heard the news on the radio.' She hesitated. 'Callum, are you all right?'

'I have to stay and do what I can to help. It's pretty bad. The emergency services are here, but there are a couple of people trapped and it's going to take some time to get them out.'

She heard a muffled voice in the background.

'Holly, I can't talk now. I'll see you later.' He said something else, something which sounded amazingly like, ''Love you.'' But it couldn't possibly have been, she knew that, then the line went dead.

Holly felt her stomach tighten. Only now, as she stared at the receiver, did she realise that he hadn't actually answered her question when she had asked if he was all right.

She put the phone down and turned slowly to find Agnes and Fiona standing in the doorway.

Holly moistened her dry lips with her tongue. 'It's the motorway pile-up. He said it's pretty bad. A couple of people are trapped and he's helping out.'

Panic surged through her, flaring out of control. Why hadn't he answered her? Suddenly she knew that something was wrong. Please, God, don't let him be hurt.

'I have to go to him. He may need help.' She was already heading for the door. 'Will you…?'

'I'll have a word with Jamie and explain as soon as he comes out with his next patient.'

Holly nodded, only half listening as she grabbed her briefcase and ran to the car.

The drive to the site of the accident seemed to take for ever. Traffic on the motorway had been brought to a halt and the effect, the silence combined with the dark, was almost eerie.

Hastily rigged emergency floodlights were trained on the wreckage that had once been several cars. One was on fire, and flames were shooting skywards, while close by smoke billowed from a lorry. There was a strong smell of something—she thought it must be petrol. She could smell it on the air, feel it in her lungs.

It was like the worst kind of nightmare and somewhere, in the middle of all that, was Callum. The thought filled her with dread.

'Sorry, miss.' A young policeman came towards her. 'I'll have to ask you to go back. You shouldn't be here. There's been a nasty accident.'

'I know. I'm a doctor. I believe one of my colleagues, Dr McLoud, is here already. How…how bad is it?'

'It's a real mess.' The man shook his head. 'I've never seen anything like it and I've seen a few. We'll be glad of all the help we can get.'

'How many casualties?' Holly asked as she began to pick her way precariously over twisted pieces of metal. The man's hand came under her arm, supporting her, and she was grateful.

'A dozen so far. One or two were minor injuries. Two dead—the rest, I don't know.' His mouth twisted into a weary line of resignation. 'Two of those were little more than kids. They looked pretty bad to me.'

As he spoke an ambulance set off, siren wailing, into the night. 'We've managed to shift most of the vehicles but the fire chaps are going to have to cut a couple of them apart. Watch out for that hose.'

His grip tightened as she slipped on a layer of foam. She drew a deep breath and coughed. 'My God, what is that smell?' She pressed a gloved hand to her nose and mouth.

'Some kind of chemicals from that tanker over there. He slid across both lanes. One of the cars hit him sideways on. The rest just kept coming. We still haven't been able to get the car driver out. God knows what sort of state he's in, but we can't move him yet. I know I wouldn't like to be in there. It's like sitting on a time bomb, waiting for this lot to go up.'

Holly stopped, gasping painfully for breath as her gaze took in the full extent of the horrifying scene. It was a miracle that anyone had survived.

Her fingers clenched into small fists and she swallowed hard. 'What about Dr McLoud? Was he involved in the crash?'

'I gather he was one of the tail-enders. Damned bad luck. I haven't seen him but someone said he had a head injury. The paramedics tried to persuade him to go to hospital but he insisted on staying with the chap in the car.'

Holly felt sick. 'He'll be glad of some help.'

'You're not thinking of going in there?'

'I brought some extra medical supplies with me. Besides, two pairs of hands are probably better than one. Can you get me in there?'

The policeman, Bryan Prentiss, looked at her. 'You do realise the whole thing could go up at any time?'

She smiled wryly. 'Then the sooner I get in there and give a hand the better, don't you think?'

He shook his head ruefully. 'I'll come with you.'

'No, better not. There's nothing you can do and we'll probably need all the space we can get. But thanks for the offer anyway.'

Somehow she managed to manoeuvre her way slowly over the twisted metal debris. It was snowing more heavily now as, shining the torch ahead of her, she made her way slowly along the length of the tanker, all the time conscious of the acrid smell of chemicals.

She gasped with horror at the sight of the small car wedged solidly beneath it. She didn't need to be an expert to see that it must have spun out of control on the wet road, making a sideways impact. The front passenger wing was crushed almost beyond recognition and part of the roof was crushed where it had come to a halt beneath the tanker.

Her foot slipped on a piece of wreckage. Gasping, she flung out a hand to save herself, sending a beam of torchlight into the window, and her heart gave a momentary lurch as she saw Callum.

He was supporting the injured man's neck and head. His face looked grey and haggard.

He drew a ragged breath as he looked at her for one long, disbelieving moment, and she told herself she must have imagined the flicker of relief she had seen etched in his features as he rasped, 'Are you crazy? What the hell are you doing here? Get the hell out of here—*now*.'

She edged closer, carefully tugging fragments of broken glass out of the window. 'I thought you might need some help.'

'Well, I don't.' His jaw was rigid with tension and she saw a thin trickle of blood seeping slowly from a wound at his temple. Her eyes blurred with sudden tears. She blinked them away, knowing that this wasn't the time to get emotional.

Reaching into her pocket for a handkerchief, she pressed it gently to the wound. 'I'm not going anywhere, Callum, so you might as well get used to the idea,' she said quietly. She eased aside the buckled door on the driver's side of the car so that she could get closer to the injured man.

'How is he?'

'Not good.' The response was terse. 'Head and neck injuries, maybe spinal—that's why I daren't move him. I've managed to get a support collar on him and given him a shot of painkiller. God knows how he's still breathing. Where the hell is that rescue team?'

'Everyone's out there, Callum, doing their best. They can't use the cutting gear until they've cleared some of the wreckage and dealt with the chemical spill.'

An oxygen mask covered the injured man's nose and mouth. He groaned softly as she pressed her fingers against his neck. 'It's all right. I'm a doctor. Just relax, we're going to get you out of here very soon.'

For the first time she was able to see the man's features clearly, and she felt her stomach tighten. He couldn't have been more than twenty. His dark hair was matted with blood, his breathing shallow and uneven.

One look at his face told her they were fighting a losing battle. If he didn't get help in the next ten minutes, she didn't think he was going to make it.

'Let me take over from you in there for a while. You must be frozen.'

Callum shook his head and the trickle of blood ran down his cheek. He used his shoulder to wipe it away. 'I can't risk moving him. I wish they'd hurry with that stretcher.'

In a lowered voice she said, 'His pulse is getting weaker. There could be serious internal injuries. How long since you gave him a painkiller?'

'I'm not sure,' Callum said raggedly. 'I'm starting to lose track of time and my watch is broken. I feel as if we've been stuck in here for ever.'

Her hand closed briefly over his. 'Just hang on in there. What did you give him?'

'Morphine. I think it must have been about an hour ago.'

'I've got some in my bag.' Easing herself carefully into the confined space, she filled a hypodermic with morphine and administered the injection. 'We don't even know his name.'

'It's Alan, Alan Brown.'

As she shivered in the darkness her hand found and briefly held Callum's. For a few seconds his gaze held hers, then she broke away. 'OK, Alan, this will help to stop the pain. You'll soon be on your way to hospital. Just hold on.'

'Get out of here, Holly,' Callum's voice rasped.

'Save your breath. I'm staying.' She glanced up at him. 'You're hurt.'

'It's nothing. I'll survive.'

'It's a deep cut. It'll probably need stitches. Have you got a headache?'

He gave a short laugh. 'What do you think?'

She eased herself carefully into the rear seat and looked at him, feeling the weak tears well up again. 'I think…' She swallowed hard on the lump in her throat. 'I don't think you're safe to be let out on your own.'

His free hand reached out, his fingers twining with hers as he eased her towards him. Instinctively she squeezed his hand. 'Are you suggesting that I need looking after?' The words came slowly, almost in a whisper.

But wasn't that Sarah's job? She closed her eyes and blinked hard, before giving a forced laugh. 'That sounds like a full-time job to me.'

'But we've got time, Holly. We've got all the time in the world.'

Except that any minute now the world might explode around them. A bubble of panic welled up, giving an edge to her voice. 'No matter what happens, I want you to know that I love you, Callum. You were right—there's a time for letting go. I've wasted so much time because I was afraid. We need to talk.'

'Oh, God…'

She froze. 'Callum, what…?' She followed his gaze and gave a tiny sob. 'They're here. Everything's going to be all right. They'll have you out of here in a few minutes.'

Moments later she was out of the car. She was vaguely aware that she was shivering and that figures were moving around them.

'OK, Doc, we'll have you out of there in no time.' The chief fire officer peered in at the shattered window. 'We've shifted the rest of the wreckage out of the way. Just hang on a few minutes longer and we'll have the young laddie out and away to hospital.'

Holly straightened. She sighed, suddenly very weary. Her head was pounding. Then Callum was standing beside her, swaying, rubbing at his arms to restore the circulation. He looked awful. In the flashing blue lights his features looked haggard.

'We'll have you in the ambulance, sir, to get that head of yours seen to.'

'There's no need,' Callum's voice grated. 'It's a cut, that's all. I'll be fine.'

The man hovered. 'It might be best just to get it looked at...'

Holly felt the muscles in Callum's arm tense. She smiled at the man and said quickly, 'It's all right, I'm a doctor. I'll take full responsibility.'

'Well, if you're sure?'

She nodded and took Callum's arm, looking up at him. 'Come on, let's go home, shall we? I think you've done your good deed for the day.'

The drive back to the cottage seemed endless. Callum sat slumped in the passenger seat, his eyes closed. She could sense the tension in him.

Cutting the engine, she tried to summon the energy to move, to get out of the car. Callum sat beside her, making no attempt to do so.

'Come on,' she said. 'I think we both need coffee.'

He drew a breath and turned his head to look at her. 'It's late.'

'I know, but I need to unwind.'

He followed her into the sitting room and stood, rubbing at his eyes. She poured two brandies.

'Hmm, strange coffee.'

'I don't know about you, Callum, but I need something stronger.' She looked at him and thought, Right now I want to be in your arms and I want to stay there for ever.

'You'd better let me take a look at that cut.' That was a mistake—it meant she had to move closer, into the danger zone. Her hand reached up and she was surprised to find that it was shaking. 'You're lucky. It needs cleaning but I don't think you'll need stitches.' Suddenly she was feeling very angry, without really knowing why.

Her mind was exhausted, shattered by the fear that she might have lost him—except that he wasn't hers to lose, and never would be.

She said briskly, 'How do you feel?'

'If you really want to know, bloody awful.'

'Well, what do you expect if you will insist on playing the hero?' she snapped ungraciously. 'Do you have any inkling of what you were up against out there? You were damn lucky, Callum, damn lucky. You do realise what could have happened—?'

She broke off, suddenly shivering violently. Only now was she beginning to realise the full enormity of it all. Taking several deep breaths, she half turned away, only to feel Callum's hands on her shoulders, preventing her.

'Holly, what's wrong?'

She couldn't believe he had to ask. He had nearly died and he wanted to know what was wrong! She looked up at him, her face taut with strain, to find him watching her, his lips set in a hard, fierce line.

'Nothing's wrong. I don't know what you mean.'

His breathing was ragged as he held her, drawing her towards him and forcing her to look into his compelling blue eyes. 'It's all right, Holly. It's over. Everything's going to be all right.'

If only she could believe that. 'Oh, Callum, I thought I'd lost you.'

His fingers caressed her cheek, stroked her hair. He was speaking softly as he held her, his own throat tightening in painful spasms. 'It's all right. Don't cry.'

'You could have been killed.' Her voice was muffled against his chest. 'I thought—'

'Don't!' His lips brushed against her mouth, silencing the words, then, before she knew what was happening, his mouth came down on hers, relentless, firm, demanding.

They clung together, Holly offering no resistance as his hands moved over her body. He raised his head briefly to look down at her. 'I need you,' he groaned softly as his mouth made advances over her throat, eyes and then back to her mouth again, claiming it with a passion that left them both breathless.

She responded with an ardour that matched his own. This was where she wanted to be. She was filled with a need to be part of him, to hold him, to keep him safe. She could feel the heat of his body through the thin sweatshirt he was wearing.

'I love you,' he rasped.

'I love you, too,' she said brokenly.

Callum gazed wonderingly into her eyes, then, almost hesitantly, drew her towards him again, smoothing her hair as she laid her head against his chest. 'I thought I must be hallucinating when you suddenly appeared out there. I'd been thinking about you, thinking what a hell of a waste—'

'No!' Gently she pressed her fingers against his mouth. 'Don't. Don't say it. I've been such a fool. I wasted so much time, I see that now.'

She had to force herself to speak through the tightness

in her throat. 'It's just that... I told myself I wouldn't let this happen again, that I could never feel this way about anyone...' Her voice broke. She looked up at him. 'I realise Sarah will always be part of your life, that you must care...'

A groan rose in his throat as he silenced her with a kiss, before raising his head to look at her. 'Holly, you're wrong. Whatever there was between Sarah and me was over long ago.' He smiled. 'I'm not even sure there *was* anything. If there was, I'm not sure it was ever love. We're friends, good friends, but that's all there is—all there will ever be.'

She stared at him, wanting desperately to believe him, but fear gave an edge to her voice. 'But she came to see you. You went to see her.'

'Sarah was confused and unhappy,' he said softly. 'The only reason she came to see me was because she was afraid.'

She stared at him. 'Afraid?'

'Of what I, and other people, friends, might think.' His grasp tightened, forcing her to look at him. 'I know what people say. They think Sarah broke our engagement to marry my best friend. It isn't true, Holly. I told you, we were never in love.'

'Callum, you don't have to—'

'I want to. You have a right to know and I want to put the record straight.' He looked at her, his hand brushing against her cheek.

'Yes, we grew up together, we spent time together, but it was never more than that. I was happy for Sarah when she decided to marry Liam. I was proud to be asked to be best man at their wedding.'

His voice roughened. 'No one could have foreseen what would happen. Two years later Liam became ill with what everyone thought was a virus, something he'd get over.

But he didn't. Two months on he was diagnosed as having leukaemia. He…died soon after.'

'Oh, my love. I'm so sorry. But…I don't understand. Why—?

'Why did Sarah come back?' He smiled. 'Because she met someone else. She didn't believe it would ever happen—she didn't want it to happen. But it did. Steve asked her to marry him, but before she'd agree Sarah felt she had to come home, to see her friends, to explain.'

'You mean, she wanted your approval.'

'If you like. Not that she needed it. The fact that she's fallen in love with Steve doesn't in any way diminish what she felt for Liam.'

'You don't have to explain,' Holly said softly. 'I've been clinging to the past too. I was afraid to let go. I couldn't see any future, especially not when…' She turned her face up to his, her eyes full of anguish. 'I thought you loved her. I thought that was why you went to see her.'

He kissed her mouth, then her eyes, then her mouth again. 'I love *you*,' he said softly. 'Only you—always you. There's just one thing…' His eyes glittered with quiet amusement.

'What's that?' She sighed, nestling contentedly against him.

'I'm fed up with being best man. Sarah's away on her honeymoon. I know I'm not looking my best right now, but…'

She looked at him and her eyes sparkled with mischief. 'Why, Dr McLoud, are you asking me to marry you?'

She reached up, her fingers twining in his hair. He drew a ragged breath before he bent his head to brush his lips against hers and look at her, his eyes glittering. 'Shall I take that as a yes, then?'

'I'll think about it.'

He drew her roughly towards him and kissed her until

they broke apart breathlessly, and he looked at her with laughter in his eyes. 'I shall have to keep kissing you until you agree, woman.'

'I'll think about it,' she said dreamily, and he kissed her again, and again, and again.

MILLS & BOON®

*M*akes
any time
special

Enjoy a romantic novel from
Mills & Boon®

Presents...™   *Enchanted*™   TEMPTATION.

Historical Romance™   ✓MEDICAL
ROMANCE®

MILLS & BOON®

MEDICAL ROMANCE™

THE COURAGE TO SAY YES by Lilian Darcy
Southshore #2 of 4

Paediatric surgeon Angus Ferguson had seen Caitlin Gray's fiancé, Scott, with another woman. Could he persuade her to see through Scott and look favourably on himself?

DOCTORS IN CONFLICT by Drusilla Douglas

The attraction between Catriona MacFarlane, the new Medical Registrar, and Michael Preston, orthopaedic surgeon, was *definitely* mutual, but when they both had such set ideas, how would they learn to compromise?

THE PERFECT TREATMENT by Rebecca Lang

Dr Abby Gibson was thrilled to discover she would be working with highly esteemed Dr Blake Contini. Although it was obvious from his warm smiling manner that Blake liked her, *something* was stopping him offering more than friendship...

PERFECT TIMING by Alison Roberts
The dawn of a new age...

Surgeon Jack Armstrong and nurse Amanda Morrison clashed horribly. It was their mutual delight in an elderly patient who would be one hundred years old on the first day of the new Millennium that brought them closer...

Available from 3rd December 1999

Celebrate the Millennium with your favourite romance authors. With so many to choose from, there's a Millennium story for everyone!

Presents...
> *Morgan's Child*
> *Anne Mather*
> On sale 3rd December 1999

Enchanted™
> *Bride 2000*
> *Trisha David*
> On sale 3rd December 1999

TEMPTATION.
> *Once a Hero*
> *Kate Hoffmann*
> On sale 3rd December 1999

> *Always a Hero*
> *Kate Hoffmann*
> On sale 7th January 2000

✓ **MEDICAL ROMANCE**™
> *Perfect Timing*
> *Alison Roberts*
> On sale 3rd December 1999

MILLS & BOON®
Makes any time special™

MILLS & BOON®

MISTLETOE
Magic

Three favourite Enchanted™ authors
bring you romance at Christmas.

Three stories in one volume:

A Christmas Romance
BETTY NEELS

Outback Christmas
MARGARET WAY

Sarah's First Christmas
REBECCA WINTERS

Published 19th November 1999

*Available at most branches of WH Smith, Tesco,
Martins, Borders, Easons, Volume One/James Thin
and most good paperback bookshops*

FREE!

2 Books
and a surprise gift!

We would like to take this opportunity to thank you for reading this Mills & Boon® book by offering you the chance to take TWO more specially selected titles from the Medical Romance™ series absolutely FREE! We're also making this offer to introduce you to the benefits of the Reader Service™ —

- ★ FREE home delivery
- ★ FREE gifts and competitions
- ★ FREE monthly Newsletter
- ★ Books available before they're in the shops
- ★ Exclusive Reader Service discounts

Accepting these FREE books and gift places you under no obligation to buy; you may cancel at any time, even after receiving your free shipment. Simply complete your details below and return the entire page to the address below. *You don't even need a stamp!*

YES! Please send me 2 free Medical Romance books and a surprise gift. I understand that unless you hear from me, I will receive 4 superb new titles every month for just £2.40 each, postage and packing free. I am under no obligation to purchase any books and may cancel my subscription at any time. The free books and gift will be mine to keep in any case.

M9EB

Ms/Mrs/Miss/Mr ....Initials...............................
                                                                BLOCK CAPITALS PLEASE

Surname..

Address..

....

....Postcode ....

Send this whole page to:
UK: The Reader Service, FREEPOST CN81, Croydon, CR9 3WZ
EIRE: The Reader Service, PO Box 4546, Kilcock, County Kildare (stamp required)

GIRL *in the* MIRROR
MARY ALICE MONROE

Charlotte Godowski and Charlotte Godfrey
are two sides to the same woman—a woman
who can trust no one with her secret. But
when fate forces Charlotte to deal with the
truth about her past, about the man she loves,
about her self—she discovers that only love
has the power to transform a scarred soul.